DIARY OF AN ADORABLE FAT GIRL

THE FIRST THREE BOOKS

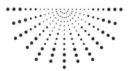

BERNICE BLOOM

DIARY OF AN ADORABLE FAT GIRL

THE FIRST THREE BOOKS

By Bernice Bloom

COPYRIGHT

BOOK ONE

BOOK ONE: Diary of an Adorable Fat Girl

1

MEETING MARY

or the love of all that is holy – what was I doing?

It was pouring down with rain and I was sheltering under a tree outside a run-down community centre in one of the less salubrious parts of Surrey. Icy cold raindrops rolled across the leaves on the branches above me before dripping onto the top of my neck and crawling slowly down my back. My shoes were so wet that my feet were forced to sit in about three inches of water.

All this because I was fat.

Sorry, I should explain – it was my first night at Fat Club. Not that they called it *Fat Club*, of course; they were far too genteel for that. Fat Club was my own special name for it. This course for very overweight people was concealed behind a title that made it sound like a jolly feature in a women's magazine. There was a battered sign hanging off the railing next to me declaring 'Six weeks to a NEW YOU. Register here.'

I didn't want to go, of course. Who would? If your choice was to spend the evening in the pub having a few glasses of wine with your mates or sit around with fat people, crying about how enormous you all are, which one are you going to choose? That's right – you'd be on your third glass of Sauvignon by now, wouldn't you?

But there I was. And it was a good thing, because an hour earlier, when I was sitting in my little flat thinking about the pizza and the bottle of wine that were taunting me from the fridge, it was touch and go whether I'd come at all. I could think of a million reasons not to come, but I'd managed to drag my large bottom off the sagging sofa, grab my coat and get on the bus.

Now all I had to do was force myself to go inside. I walked towards the door, stumbling on exposed roots and slipping on soggy leaves in the semi-darkness. The broken street light directly outside the centre made the experience particularly dismal. I felt around for the cold, wet handle. Finally, I found it and the door creaked as I turned it. It was like I was in some low-budget, 1950s horror film.

Inside, things were considerably brighter. In fact, the fluorescent lighting strips were so overpowering you could perform major heart surgery in there. I narrowed my eyes, squinting as I adjusted to the brightness, like a small woodland creature coming up from its burrow into daylight.

"Hello, welcome, welcome, welcome," said woman with a wide, smiling face and ears that stuck out through a plethora of unruly curls. She introduced herself as Liz, explaining that she was the course tutor as she reached out a large hand and pulled me into her, hugging me warmly. "Sorry if my outfit's a bit bright, I love colourful clothes."

She wasn't joking. If I were being very unkind, I'd say she was dressed in the manner of a four-year-old who's been told she can choose what she wants to wear to a party. She was wearing a very tight (I mean – so tight, you could see the outline of her major internal organs) pink dress, with red tights and a red cardigan, and had lashings of vibrant green eyeshadow thickly painted onto her eyelids. She wore a baby pink lipstick but most of that appeared to be on her teeth and chin rather than her lips so she looked like she'd been eating raspberries straight from the bush without using her hands. She even had glitter on her temples. She was a pair of butterfly wings away from winning the prize for best dressed little girl at the party.

The childlike nature of her makeup was in contrast to her stature. She was a tall and sturdy woman, carrying quite a few extra pounds.

"I'm glad you've decided to join us," she said. "I hope this class will help you change your life for the better. You know, I've lost 13 stone since I first came to the group."

"Wow, well done," I said. The generous side of me thought – that is really impressive. The less generous side thought – blimey, how fat were you before? I decided not to share the more ungenerous thought. In fact, I decided not to share any of the ungenerous thoughts I was having about her. I was being a real bitch. Sorry if you think me offensive. I'm not normally like this, but I was stressed as hell – I wanted to be at home with pizza and wine, not discussing my food issues with random strangers. I tend to go wildly on the attack when I'm under pressure.

"Take a seat," said Liz, leading me to a circle of chairs, and making the compulsory British observations about the weather. We agreed it was miserable and much colder than it normally was for the time of year (I don't know how people remember that sort of thing. Do they keep notes or something? I can't remember what the weather was like last week, let alone last year. I guess she was right though, so I nodded and smiled, raising my eyebrows in agreement with her). There were only two other people in the room – an older man and woman who barely looked up. They were tucked into a corner, wearing matching navy blue anoraks and trying to sink into the background. I tried to smile at them but they didn't smile back. Liz saw me trying to make a connection with them and gave me an enormous grin, revealing just how much lipstick she had smeared across her teeth. I'd rather have been anywhere else on earth.

"My name's Mary," I said, eventually, when the weight of the silence became too much for me to bear. I walked over and shook hands with the two older people. They didn't offer their names, so I returned to my seat, slightly cross that they didn't have the decency to pretend to be interested in me, but also happy that I'd done my bit for group relations. I've never liked to see people looking sad, and those two looked nigh on suicidal. I discovered later that their names were Phil and Philippa.

The Phils and I were sitting down with chairs between us, and as other people filtered in they took the free chairs. A woman called Janice sat to the left of me. She clutched her handbag and whimpered, "I want to go home," which endeared me to her.

"Me too, sister," I said.

What she also had in her favour, as far as our future friendship was concerned, was that she was a lot larger than me. This gave me a strange sense of confidence and happiness. I know that was selfish, and very uncharitable, but I really didn't want to be the fattest person at Fat Club. I mean – no one wants to be the fattest person at Fat Club.

"What on earth is that woman wearing?" she said, after Liz had been over to give her a welcome hug. "I didn't realise it was fancy dress."

Opposite me there was a very beautiful woman who had just come striding into the room and was preparing to sit next to the Phils. She was tall and quite big but nothing like as fat as the rest of us: size 16, at a guess. Unnervingly elegant in cream, three-quarter length trousers and a white shirt, she also had a treasure trove of gold accessories to bring the outfit to life. She looked exactly like Kelly Brook. She had no place at a Fat Club, and I longed for bouncers to appear clutching scales and a tape measure and throw her out for not reaching the required obesity level.

Liz wandered over to her, and for one insane moment I thought she was going to do exactly that – chuck the poor woman out because her stomach was too small and her thighs didn't rub together. But, instead, she told her she was very welcome, hugged her, and invited her to sit down. I watched the alarm spread across the woman's face as she released herself from the compulsory hug she'd just endured and took in Liz's outfit. "My name's Veronica," she said. "I don't know whether I should be here. I used to be a model."

"Everyone's welcome, regardless of who they are or who they used to be. We're simply here to support one another. Why don't you stay and see how you feel," said Liz.

"OK," said Veronica. Liz moved away and the glamourpuss smiled at me, revealing perfect teeth. I smiled back, making sure I didn't show mine.

The club was quite a long way from my home. Living on the other side of town meant it was quite a trek to get over there, but I couldn't risk going to a club near to my house in case someone saw me. It's bad enough being fat without advertising it to all your friends and family. I'd never have lived it down if my boss at the garden centre had seen me walking into a local club. Keith's always been a bit of a clown and would have found it very amusing to mock my efforts to lose weight.

"While we're waiting for the others to get here, does anyone have any questions?" said Liz. "I know you must be wondering about the course and how it works."

"Yes, I'd like to know that." I raised my hand a little, like a child in school. "How does it work? What do we do? How are we all going to lose tonnes of weight? And how quickly will we lose it?" I could hear the urgency and desperation in my own voice. It didn't sound pretty!

"We will obviously go into that in great detail later." Liz gave a warm smile. "But – briefly – this course is about dealing with your issues psychologically, not physically. When you're ready to diet and exercise, you will."

"OK." I was trying to stay positive but this sounded like a load of New Age bullshit. "I'm really ready to lose the weight, now. I'm sick of being fat. I'd like to get thinner as quickly as possible."

"Amen, sister," said Janice, and I treated her to the biggest smile I could muster.

"OK. I get it, I really do. You desperately want to lose weight, but let's look at the facts," she said calmly, perhaps sensing that I wasn't entirely sold on all this. "You know what you have to do to lose weight, don't you? You know that by increasing exercise and cutting back on your calorie intake you will lose weight. Right?"

"Right," I said.

"But you're not doing it."

"No, I think we can all agree on that." I rubbed my fat stomach and let the ripples provide the evidence.

"Why not?" she asked.

"Um. I don't know." I felt myself go scarlet and wished I'd never asked a bloody question in the first place. I wished I was at home with a bottle of wine.

"Look, I don't want to embarrass you at all, I'm just trying to explain that losing weight is actually quite a complicated psychological shift, if you want to keep it off, so that takes a bit of time."

She looked at me and I was sure she could sense the disappointment and frustration emanating from me.

"There must be a reason you're not cutting back on your calories and losing weight, mustn't there? Or you'd do it. Something's stopping you, and it's not something physical – no one's standing in your way at the gym and not allowing you onto the treadmill, or forcing you to eat cake. It's something psychological, and that's what we have to sort out.

"This course is to try and understand all the mental processes that we go through as overeaters. It will involve working out why you eat too much in the first place. This is a gentle, kind environment and within it we'll explore your emotions and learn to understand them."

What she said made perfect sense, of course, but I still didn't get it...not *really*. How would I be filled with positive energy and never eat anything but celery ever again merely by chatting about how fat I was?

"Will you just trust me?" said Liz. "Stay with this and I promise you – I can help you."

"OK," I said, though I had my reservations about trusting her. I didn't trust anyone, not really. My ability to trust had deserted me along with my innocence all those years ago.

I looked up to see a man walk in; he was one of those very jolly fat guy types – all smiles and laughter and cracking jokes. He didn't seem to fit into this rather dull group. He sat down to the right of me and I sighed inwardly. I was starting to think I might get an empty seat next to me, which I'd have liked. I hoped he wasn't going to try and jolly me up...no sing-alongs or hand holding or anything nasty like that.

"Am I in the right place?" His voice was barely a whisper. "I am looking for Overeaters Anonymous. How will I know when I find it? You're too thin to be in the group I'm looking for."

It was a valiant attempt at humour in the face of embarrassment, and I did appreciate the compliment, so I smiled at him as he sat down. He took off his glasses that had steamed up when he came into the warm building, and wiped them on his checked shirt. He had odd facial hair – not just a simple beard, but a sort of complicated moustache/beard combo that had been shaved into place. Like topiary.

There were six of us in the room when Liz decided to start the session. She was expecting 10, she said, but it was already 10 minutes late and she didn't want to keep us waiting.

"I bet they've only got the hall booked for 90 minutes," whispered the man. "Then the 'Under-Eaters Anonymous' group arrive, and they can't risk us all being in the same room at the same time."

I smiled at him. He was ever so slightly bonkers which cheered me up.

I heard Janice giggling to herself at the man's joke. "That's right; the under-eaters are terrified of the overeaters," she said. "They're worried we might eat them."

Liz began by talking about the importance of us working together as group, and how we must contact one another during the week. She said she'd give out a list of numbers and we should send a text to the person on our left during the week, just to encourage them.

The very smiley, happy, red-faced man with the steamed-up glasses and odd facial hair arrangement gave me a smile. "I'm Ted. I'll text you to check you're OK. Just call me if you need to talk or anything," he said in a kind voice.

"Thank you," I replied, and I instantly regretted judging him on the beard thing.

"I'll text you," I said to Janice.

"WILL I HAVE TO PUT MY BAG OF CHIPS DOWN TO REPLY," SHE SAID. I assured her that there was no need of that. "Let's not take this too seriously, Janice," I said, and she gave me a lovely big smile.

7

I guess Janice was about mid-40s…certainly older than me. I'd only just turned 30. She was quite plain-looking, with short brown hair and very little makeup, but she had such mischief in her eyes that I could imagine men really being attracted to her. At a guess, I would say she was a size 24, but she wore it well.

"Ted, why don't you lead us off by telling the group something about yourself and why you're here today," said Liz.

"Oh, OK," he said with an embarrassed shrug. He had turned the colour of ham.

We were all watching him and thinking 'Thank God I don't have to go first.'

Liz sensed his concern, or perhaps she was just worried about the strange colour he'd turned. Either way, she stepped in.

"Look, you don't have to if you don't want to, but I want everyone in the group to understand one another and be aware of each other's problems. I think it will help you when you're away from the sessions, in terms of offering support to one another, if you have an understanding of each other's issues."

"Sure," he said in a voice which suggested he'd never been less sure of anything in his life. He stood up.

"OK, here we go then. I never used to have problems. In fact I used to be a very good sportsman," he said, and I immediately looked up. I'd been a good sportswoman myself many years ago, but I certainly wasn't going to tell them anything about that. I'd never told anyone about the awful things that had happened to me when I was younger.

Ted continued to explain that his life had involved playing county rugby, having trials with a range of top English clubs, and being thought of as a future international.

"It was my life," he said. "All I could think of was that first England cap. I'd dream about it and build it up into a colourful scenario in my mind. It was like playing for England was the only thing worth doing. Nothing else mattered."

But a call-up to the national squad never happened. A freak injury ended his career just when he was on the verge of greatness. Ted told us about the moment a scrum collapsed on him and he lay on the floor unable to move.

"Do you all know what a scrum is?" he asked. "Without being too technical, it's when the biggest players on the pitch all pile in together to get the ball. The opposition sides push against one another, ramming their shoulders in against their opposition number. It's quite OK if it's done properly, but I was pushing at an awkward angle and I twisted, and ended dumped down on the ground neck first. We all winced in support.

"I was only 22," he said. "I fell into a great depression afterwards about not being able to play any more. I knew I should be grateful to be alive. Certainly when they took me off the pitch, the doctors were very concerned about whether I'd ever walk again, or lead a normal life. My mum says no one knew whether I'd live or die. I *was* grateful to the doctors for everything they did. I'm grateful to them today – 10 years on since the accident – and will be forever more. But I was also desperately sad, and felt like my world had collapsed. I couldn't cope without playing the sport that had defined me, and was creating a future for me. All I'd ever wanted to be was an international rugby player. I felt as if my past, my present and future had all been snatched away.

"I became useless. Everything felt futile when I couldn't play sport any more. I tried to eat my way out of sadness, but that didn't work. We all know that doesn't work. I ate more and felt sadder and ate more, and felt sadder still, now I'm morbidly obese and I look at the pictures of me playing rugby and that feels like another person. I can't play rugby again, but I'd like to be more like the person in the pictures."

Ted stopped and I reached up to touch his arm, to express sympathy and display solidarity. I knew nothing about rugby, but I knew about the pressures of sport and I knew about overeating. I understood exactly how food could wrap you in its comforting facade and refuse to let you go.

There was a big round of applause when Ted had finished…the sort of clapping that said: 'We're with you, we totally understand.' I looked over at him and smiled; he blushed a little, then gave me the biggest smile ever.

Next came Janice. She stood up. "I have a similar story," she said, before correcting herself quickly. "Well, not similar – I wasn't a brilliant rugby player or anything like that. What I mean is that I was OK until something major happened. Things were good, life was ticking along, then my mum died."

Janice took a deep breath. She was finding it hard. "Sorry," she kept saying as she stuttered and breathed heavily, attempting to tell her story. "It was years ago that it happened, just after my 40th birthday, so I don't know why it still affects me so badly today, you'd think I'd be used to it by now, but you never really get used to it. I'm not sure the pain of missing her has got any easier, I've just got used to the pain being there. This is bringing it all back to the surface. It's difficult."

"Of course it's difficult, and you're doing really well," said Liz. "You're in the best, most supportive company here today." As Liz said that, I realised what pressure there was on the rest of us to look after one another.

"Mum died and I lost all control," she continued. "I mean – *all* control – I just ate and ate and ate, and then I ate some more."

Janice dissolved into tears.

"You've done really well," said Liz, stroking Janice's shaking back. "Could you go next please, Mary?"

"Me?"

"Yes please, Mary, if you don't mind? I think Janice needs to sit down now."

"Right. Um. I don't know what to say," I said, standing up and looking down at the scuffed wooden floor that reminded me so much of school. "I'm embarrassed and ashamed to be this size, and I wish this wasn't me here in a church hall talking about how fat I am. I wish I was out with my friends having a lovely time, or flirting with the guy who lives in the flat underneath mine, because he's bloody gorgeous. You should see him – honestly, he's lovely. Way too lovely for me. Christ, you should see the lovely women he brings back with him. But, anyway. Um. Where was I?"

"Just talk us through your issues with food," Liz said gently.

"I guess I'm fat because whenever I feel low or vulnerable, I eat."

"OK," said Liz. "So you're using food to comfort you? You're convincing yourself that food is the answer to emotions that are stirred up, even when those emotions aren't hunger?"

"Yes. That's right. I know deep down that I'm not hungry when someone gets cross with me or laughs at me or makes me feel horrible, but eating sure makes whatever the real feelings are go away."

"Does it though?" asked Liz. "Or is eating just a temporary relief, and then the next time you feel low, you do the same thing?"

"Every time I feel low I eat."

"So it's not really solving any problems then?"

"No," I said. "None at all."

"OK, Mary. You're doing really well. Is there anything else you'd like to share? Perhaps about your past, and when the overeating started?"

"I did sport when I was younger like Ted. I was a gymnast. You wouldn't believe that now, would you? Gymnastics was a hard sport. I don't want to blame the way I am now on it or anything, but it's tough to spend your whole adolescence running around in a leotard and having to perform and then be marked out of 10. I guess it leaves you feeling like you're always being judged.

"Also some things happened when I was younger. I mean – one thing in particular happened. I guess it's always haunted me a bit. I haven't always been fat. I started putting on weight when I was about 20, years after stopping gymnastics but probably because of the thing that happened, but maybe not. I don't know really.

"Before that, things were different... I was always the successful one... I know it's hard to believe it now, but I was always the prettiest girl, the fittest girl, the best at school. I was the pretty blonde gymnast who all the boys fancied, then I put on a bit of weight and I was the curvaceous blonde ex-gymnast who'd retired rather suddenly, then in my early 20s I became the fat blonde, now I'm just a morbidly obese lump on legs and I'd be amazed if anyone even noticed my hair colour."

"Don't be daft," said Ted, sounding genuinely moved. "You're beautiful. Everyone can see that." There were general murmurings of approval for Ted's kind words and I smiled at him before carrying on.

"I guess I put enormous pressure on myself to be perfect, and every time things go wrong I turn to food. That's what we all do, isn't it? As you get older more things go wrong so you eat more. Then being fat becomes a problem in its own right, so you eat even more because you feel awful about being fat and you need comforting, and the problem exacerbates, and you feel like a complete idiot because your reaction to a problem is feeding the problem and making it worse every day.

"Now I'm standing here in front of you and I seem to have eaten myself into a life I don't want to be in any more, and I don't really know how to get out of it. I feel very ashamed a lot of the time. I'm so ugly and fat I hate to go out, but it's depressing to stay in when all your friends are out. So you eat. You eat because somewhere inside it feels like the answer to everything…and the problems just grow. Sorry, I'm repeating myself…but that's what happens."

"Well done, Mary," said Liz. "You mentioned that something had happened that you thought might be the cause of your overeating. Something when you were a gymnast, was it? Would you like to share that?"

"No, no," I said. "The only thing is that I eat too much. That's the only 'thing'. That's all I wanted to say."

"OK," said Liz. "Don't worry. Another time, perhaps."

I sat down and Ted leaned over and lightly touched my hands that were resting in my lap, it was a warm gesture and surprisingly touching after the stress of having to talk to everyone. "You're going to do this," he said. "And – please believe me – you are not ugly at all, you're very pretty."

I smiled at him and squeezed his hand a little. No one had said anything like that to me for about a decade.

They were the sort of words that I'd always fantasised about Dave, my gorgeous neighbour, saying to me but all Dave wanted to do was fondle my tits. Sorry, I know that's crude, but it's the truth. More of that later.

After me came Phil, the older man opposite. Phil was huge – be must have been six foot six inches and about 25 stone (I'm guessing here – I find it very difficult to guess what men weigh – all I know is that he was super-enormous). He had receding white hair and he scratched his bald patch nervously. I think he was the one I felt most sorry for. His shyness was crippling and he really didn't want to talk. He still had his anorak on, zipped up to his neck, when he stood up and mumbled about how difficult he was finding everything, then how he didn't like to talk in front of strangers.

"Just tell us about something you like. Anything at all," tried Liz.

"I like Star Wars," he said, before turning and heading back to his seat.

I felt myself shift a little in my seat. My heart beat a little faster.

"You OK?" asked Ted.

"Sure," I replied.

"You've gone pale," he said.

"It's nothing. It's just that I absolutely hate the theme from *Star Wars*. HATE it."

"Right," he replied, uncomprehendingly. "I'll remember never to play it at Fat Club."

"Philippa, would you like to go next?" asked Liz, smiling warmly at the woman who I assumed was Phil's wife.

"I won't, thanks," she said, blushing to the roots of her tightly permed, grey hair. It seemed a shame. None of us wanted to share our innermost fears and complexities with a group of overweight strangers and I confess I held back on a lot of my story, but the point of all this was to allow us to bond with one another, support one another and identify with one another so it was important to say something, if not everything. With every story I heard, I was feeling less of a 'freak'. Not totally unfreaky – I wouldn't go that far – but definitely less freaky. That had to be something, surely?

Next came Veronica. She stood up to reveal a body that was so far from fat that it was ridiculous. It was the body we all wanted. Not tiny, by any means, but these things are relative – she certainly wasn't fat like the rest of us.

"I know I'm not huge," she said, clearing her throat as she looked around the room. Her long, wavy dark hair tumbled over her shoulders. "I appreciate there are a lot of people here who are much larger." I'm sure she looked at me as she said that. "But I'm a lot fatter than I've ever been in my life before and I feel totally out of control around food. It doesn't matter what size you are if you feel uncomfortable and hate your body.

"I was a model for seven years. You consume nothing but Diet Coke some days, and an apple if you're lucky. I spent the best part of a decade feeling starving all the time, and eating cotton wool to curb the worst of the hunger pangs. I gave up modelling at 22 when the work started drying up and realised that I didn't know how to eat. I don't understand how to control myself because I never had to when I wasn't eating. The weight piled on. I've put on six stone since I gave up. Six stone. Can you imagine that?"

I can't have been alone in thinking that she must have been painfully thin before.

"We can help you. We can help you all." Liz looked around at her six chicks with maternal pride. "Now then, everybody up." She clapped her hands loudly, making Phil jump out of his seat. Either he was particularly sensitive or he was half-asleep. I couldn't rule out either option, to be honest.

"Into pairs please, and I want you to talk about why you decided to come here today."

I turned to Ted and asked him whether he'd like to be my partner. He looked remarkably pleased, smiling and glowing red.

"So, why did you come here?" he asked.

"Because I realised I couldn't cross my legs properly," I replied, and I watched his eyebrows raise and a look of confusion spread across his face.

It sounded very silly, but it was the truth. When I realised I couldn't cross my legs, I knew that I wasn't just a few pounds over fighting weight but I was seriously, undeniably and horribly fat. It wasn't a pleasant realisation.

There had been plenty of other unpleasant developments over the years, as I'd piled on the pounds. Moments when I was driven to consuming nothing but shakes for a week or proteins for a fortnight, or eating a lemon every morning – wincing and gagging as the bitterness swamped my mouth. Lots of times when I'd not been able to look in the mirror in the changing room because the sight of myself struggling into a pair of size 20 trousers, when all the evidence was that a 22 would be ambitious, was too much to bear. Every fat girl has cried in a changing room.

But the leg crossing thing was different. The fact that I couldn't sit in a comfortable position made me feel like I was deformed in some way – or to put it a different way: *I had deformed myself in some way.* I'd shoved so much food into my mouth that I was unable to function normally – I couldn't sit down properly. Who would do that to herself? I was young, fit, healthy and moderately attractive. I had all the advantages that life could throw at me, but I'd put so much food into my mouth that I'd turned myself into a creature unable to walk any distance without panting like an elderly, chain-smoking marathon runner, and now I couldn't sit down properly either. What was I supposed to do – lie down all day? No – I know what you're thinking – what I was supposed to do was get out there and lose some weight.

And I tried. My God, I tried. I tried to exercise more, but my thighs rubbed together when I walked, leaving me so bloody sore and tender that only the application of a bag of frozen peas would calm the redness. No one tells you these things when they're serving you cakes, do they?

Why don't they tell you that a simple walk anywhere will give you such chaffing that it will feel as if someone had taken to your inner thighs with a cheese grater? And that's the trouble with getting fat. The very act of being fat presents, in itself, a whole host of side effects which make losing the fat wildly difficult.

Let's look at the evidence:

'Walk more.'

NOT POSSIBLE: YOUR ANKLES GET SORE AND YOUR THIGHS RUB TOGETHER like sandpaper.

'Join a gym.'

Oh yeah, right. Join a gym and wobble around for two minutes on the treadmill before collapsing in an indecorous heap? You need to be fit to join a gym – everyone knows that.

'Go swimming.'

Are you insane? Really – are you? In the interests of public decency it's impossible to wear a swimming costume. Christ.

BEFORE TOO LONG, THE ONLY EXERCISE AVAILABLE TO ME WOULD BE rolling.

Eating less would have been one way of solving the problem, but that didn't work. I don't say that flippantly – everyone who has an eating disorder knows that they can't eat less like they can't breathe less or shiver less when cold. You have no control over it. Or you think you have no control over it, which is exactly the same thing.

I went to talk to my GP on the offchance that he would have a miracle cure tucked up his sleeve.

"I need to lose weight," I told him.

It turned out he agreed wholeheartedly. He even measured me and weighed me and yes, confirmed that, indeed, I did need to lose weight. Quite a lot of weight, as it happens. But he had no exciting pills to give me that would help. "Eat less; exercise more," he said. Thanks, doc, revolutionary advice.

"You OK?" asked Ted.

"Yes," I said. "Just thinking – it's all really weird this, isn't it? I mean – thinking about why we are here? Trying to articulate it beyond saying 'because I want to lose weight'."

"My dear, it's because we are so dreadfully, dreadfully fat," he replied in a funny voice that made me laugh quite a lot.

"Well, yes, there certainly is that," I replied.

"It would be wrong of you to deny it." He rubbed his stomach so it all shook like a giant jelly. "We're fat and we can't hide it, so we need to change it."

He was right that you can't hide it. The horrible thing about eating too much is that everybody knows you have a problem. You can't deny that you're a food addict. You could be a drug addict without people necessarily knowing, certainly until you did yourself real damage, no one would know. The same with alcoholics. It doesn't show until you're really badly affected by it. That's not the same with overeaters, we get fatter and fatter and fatter and everyone knows that we are eating too much, and everyone is wondering why we don't just cut down.

There's so much judgement of fat people because we're completely out of control around something that everybody else can manage. From the littlest babies to the oldest pensioners, we all eat. But there are some of us who can't control how and when we eat. It seems ridiculous. Of all the problems in the world, all the big things going on, we idiots in that room couldn't stop putting food into our mouths even though it was killing us.

At least now we had each other. It was us against the world – we were valiant, fat, fighting soldiers. And we would stick together and help each other.

I left the meeting feeling pretty bloody wonderful. Really good. I thought the six-week course might get me on track, I could lose a stone in that time, and start moving more. I vowed to get off the bus a stop early, drink more water, and make the small changes that would create a real difference. Christ, I was on top of this. I could sort it out.

But the journey home was quite long, and the more I sat there, the more my mind dwelled on things. It was desperate: why did I have to eat nothing but lettuce for the next two years? Why had I got this fat in the first place? I'd never lose it; who was I kidding, thinking that I could? I'd tried so many times and it hadn't worked, what was so different this time? I watched the world go past from the lower deck of the R49 and felt increasingly sorry for myself. Why did I have this problem and others didn't? Happy, smiley, slim men and women got on and off the bus. It seemed so unfair. They were the sort of people who could open a packet of biscuits and just have one. Why could they do that and I couldn't? I was never going to lose weight, why was I even kidding myself?

I stepped off the bus, close to my house, and passed the fish and chip shop on the corner. The waft of vinegar flew out on the night air, its rapacious claws grabbing me around the throat. This is what happens; what always happens. Food has talons...even the smell of food has talons that tear, scratch, seize, and pull at me so I can't escape. The thought of the warmth and comfort of food is so much more powerful than the thought of being thin. Vanity's tentacles are much less sharp than those attached to the comforts of eating.

"Hi, can I get two large portions of chips, please? For me and the kids."

"Sure."

"Actually, you better make it three – my husband will be home soon."

Except there was no husband, no children at home waiting for their chips – just a small, empty flat for me to trundle into and gorge myself until I felt like crying. God, I'm lonely. I'm really lonely. I wish someone loved me.

"Actually, could you add on a portion of chips and curry sauce?"

This is the thing with being an overeater. I didn't go into the chip shop because I fancied a couple of chips. If that were the case I'd have eaten a couple of chips and gone on my merry way and all would have been fine. No – it was different from that – it was like something switched in my brain when I was around food and I had to keep eating and filling myself until I was so full that I really hurt. It was like I was mentally unwell around food. Like I hated myself through food, but I didn't really know why. I was hoping I'd find out on the course, but that night all I was finding out was that things hadn't changed at all – I needed to feel full up to cover the pain inside...the pain that I could tell no one about. The pain that was caused by the thing that happened so long ago and still hurt so much.

The shop next door sold bottles of wine that went so nicely with chips, then it was off up the street, already tearing the chip paper off and feeling the warmth of the steam rise to bite my hand. I took the chips and fed them into my mouth even though they were piping hot and burnt my tongue as I strode towards my flat. They were also slimy and hot to the touch so I was moving them between my cupped hands to cool them down, then shoving them into my mouth. I was covered in grease, had a mouth full of piping hot chips and oil all over my face.

That was when Dave from the flat below pulled up and walked to the gate next to me. He was with a very beautiful girlfriend who didn't look like she'd ever had a chip in her life. She was wearing a stunning white mini dress. I never wear white, and I never wear minis. I looked down at my dowdy, old-lady clothes, wondering where I could dump the chips before she saw them.

"OK?" asked Dave.

"Sure," I said, spitting bits of fried potato out as I spoke.

"This is Felicity." I looked over at the vision of feminine beauty and smiled. I couldn't offer her my hand because it was full of chips, so I just looked wistfully as she put out her tiny little hand, then withdrew it when she realised I wouldn't be shaking it. Meanwhile Dave wiped bits of chip off the side of his face.

Eventually, he looked from the bag of chips to my handful of chips to my mouth and smiled.

"Enjoy your supper. See you soon."

His girlfriend wiggled into his flat and I waddled into mine.

Fuck it. Fuck all of it.

2

WEEK TWO AT FAT CLUB

I used to be elegant, you know. Properly nice, with cheekbones and ankles and things. I used to wear my hair up. That's a tell-tale sign of a woman with confidence – when she'll happily pull her fringe back into a clip, or twist the back of her hair up into a chignon. You know what these women are saying? These women are crying, 'I can pull my hair back and let you see more of my face because I'm not deeply ashamed of what my face looks like.'

Me? I pull it all forward over my face, hoping to hide my puffy cheeks and jowly jawline as much as possible. If I could wear it pulled forward over my face covering it entirely, I would. But then I wouldn't be able to see and I'd bump into people. Nobody wants a fat woman with hair all over her face bumping into them. So I don't pull it forward, but I don't tie it back either. Do you see how complicated this all is? It's hard being fat. Don't get fat. It's a pain.

It was quite difficult persuading myself to go back to Fat Club for the second week.

I had left there the week before feeling so inspired, but after my chip disaster, I'd woken up feeling terrible. This is the trouble with reaching out for help – if you make the effort and it doesn't work, you feel worse than ever. I felt crushed; like I'd tried and failed; like nothing could help me. Before I made the effort to ask for help, I could relax in the knowledge that there might be a solution out there. Now it felt as if I'd proven to myself that there was no solution: no help, no hope and no point in trying to convince myself otherwise.

After that dreadful night, the rest of the week did get better, but I certainly didn't feel any different as a result of the course. Going into my job in Fosters DIY & Garden Centre, I was as aware as ever of people around me eating food: food in shops and food on posters. Food made me feel nice. Why couldn't I have food?

Then I'd go through the process of reminding myself why: because my face was slowly drowning in a pool of fat; all my clothes had gone up six sizes and even my shoes. Shoes! What was that all about? Feet don't get fat. Except mine did. I didn't know whether they were fatter, or whether the pressure exerted on them by the weight of my heavy torso flattened them out. Either way – not good. Not to be recommended.

I'd remind myself that I couldn't bend over since I got fat...not really. That's a horrible thing. The feeling you get when you reach down to tie up your shoes is horrific. Your stomach is in the way and pushes back on your internal organs. You can't breathe. You feel light-headed, as if you're about to faint or be sick. As if, to be honest, you're going to die. I'd come up from a basic shoe tie or sock on-put with my face the colour of sun-dried tomato, whining and puffing like I'd just run a marathon dressed as a polar bear.

The day before the second session, Ted sent me a text saying how much he was looking forward to seeing me at Fat Club. "Well this week it's been an absolute bloody disaster for me," he said. "If you want to see what a very fat man looks like when he eats marshmallows all week and gets even fatter, I suggest you come on Tuesday night. Looking forward to seeing you X."

I laughed out loud when I read it and replied to say I was looking forward to seeing him too. I decided to send a text to Janice.

"Looking forward to seeing you on Tuesday night," I wrote. "I'll be the really fat one who hasn't managed to stop eating chips all week."

Janice replied: "Your chips are nothing compare to my chocolate cake. See you Tuesday."

They call it gallows humour, don't they? That grim and ironic humour you find in a desperate or hopeless situation. I suggest we call this Marshmallows Humour: witticisms born out of the desperation of trying to lose weight. Still, at least by replying to everyone I was now committed to going to back to Fat Club.

When I walked in, I saw Ted straight away. He gave me a cheery smile and a wave, and came over to me.

"Thank you for your text," I said. "It really made me laugh."

"You have to laugh about these things, don't you?" he said. "Hard to know what else to do."

"Have you been OK this week?" I asked.

"Kind of terrible," he said. "I just don't seem to be able to sort myself out. I rang Liz in the end because I kept bingeing. Liz said it was only natural, after we'd bared our souls in class we would probably want comforting and our choice of comforting would be food. Today she's going to talk about other ways to comfort ourselves."

"That makes sense. I couldn't stop eating either," I said. "Especially straight after the class, which didn't make me feel great. In fact it made me feel as if this whole thing was such a hopeless battle. I wasn't going to come back until I got your text."

Ted blushed. "Wow. Then I'm *so* glad I sent it."

All six of us were there for the second session. Liz looked at us proudly, as if we were all four-year-olds who had just completed our 50m swimming badges. She was wearing a dress with more flowers on it than there are in the whole of Kew Gardens. Her shoes were red.

"You have all come back," she said. "That's a very good start. Mary, how have you got on this week?"

I really wish she hadn't started with me. I didn't want to kick the whole thing off with such negativity.

"I've been fine," I lied. I looked at Ted out the corner of my eye and I could see him smiling at me.

"Talk us through how you've been fine?" said Liz.

"Well, nothing terrible has happened… No major disasters," I said. "I'm still alive and all that."

"How have you got on with your eating?"

"Oh that? No, that's been terrible," I said, and heard a laugh go around the room.

"Don't worry. Tell me why it's been terrible."

"I just feel like such a failure all the time," I said. "I find myself eating without really knowing I'm doing it, and without meaning to, and I feel such an idiot that I am unable to control myself. After coming here last week I thought things would be different, then on the bus home I started to get so depressed about what an uphill task it was, and how much weight I had to lose, that I lost all my motivation in one second."

"And how did this manifest itself?"

"I bought everything in the chip shop and started eating it all before I'd even walked through the front door, then felt guilty about it, and disgusted with myself. I don't know – I felt horrible all week. The only way I could stop myself from feeling horrible was to eat. It wasn't great, really."

"Thank you for being so honest," said Liz. "What's happened to you last week is very typical and I promise you we can sort it out, so don't worry. You were scuppered by the voices in your head telling you that it was too complicated to try to lose weight. The voices said that you could never do it and it was pointless trying. Am I right?"

"Yes," I said. I hate it when people talk about voices in your head, as if you're some psycho maniac who is about to kill everybody, but she was right about the feeling I had…that this was all pointless and I was wasting my time.

"One key thing we are going to work on today is controlling the negative voices in your head. You can't let them decide your actions out of fear. You have to make choices out of confidence and positivity have to own them, understand them, be bigger than them and louder than them, then you CAN be in control of them. That's something we'll work on later. We'll also look at why you are all eating when you need comforting, rather than doing something more constructive.

Why food? We'll discuss that. For now, though, thank you, Mary, please don't worry and think it's all hopeless and helpless. It isn't. Not by a long way. You've only just started – just trust that you'll get there. We are all here to help you and we will."

I felt a tear run down my face as she spoke. It was astonishing how emotional all this was becoming. It was lovely to have someone who cared. Really cared. Cared so much they were trying to help. I know it was her job but she still seemed to care rather than criticise, and that was nice.

It also helped that not many in the group had had a particularly wonderful week (I know that sounds really selfish, but I've got to be honest – if they'd all arrived having lost half a stone each, the voices in my head would have been telling me to murder them).

I left the session feeling confident, understanding why I was reaching for food, and determined not to be undone by the voices. I just needed to get myself home without going via the chip shop.

"Fancy a drink?" said Ted.

"Oh I'd like that too," said Janice, overhearing Ted's question to me.

Once Janice said she'd like to go, I was in. I wouldn't have fancied going for a drink on my own with Ted. I mean, he was very nice and everything, but a bit too jolly and happy ALL THE TIME.

We retired to the Shipmate's Arms, just down the road from the centre, all of us waddling in a line. I wondered whether people were looking at us, and thinking that we must have come from Fat Club. I wondered whether it was a fun thing to do locally – to look for the Fat Club people trooping into the pub.

Ted went to the bar, and got me a white wine spritzer, and I sat down next to Janice, and shared my theory with her.

"It's depressing, isn't it?" she said. "I hate being fat. I wish I had a gambling problem or an overspending problem, then at least it wouldn't be blatantly obvious to everyone in the world."

"Unless you gambled away all your money and ended up living in a cardboard box somewhere. Then it would be obvious," I said, but I knew what she meant. On a daily basis I felt stupid for being so overweight.

"I'm just fed up of being a fat fuck," said Janice. "Fed up of the insults and the way it dominates my life. Fed up with looking dreadful, feeling dreadful and people treating me like I'm dreadful. I'm fed up of all of it. Nothing is nice when you're as fat as I am…nothing at all."

"Here we go" said Ted, returning to the table and putting my drink in front of me before I had the chance to reply to Janice. Ted had a pint, I had a spritzer and Janice had gone for a sparkling water. As soon as I saw Janice's drink, I realised that I should have done the same.

"You've done well…having water. Good self-control." I hoped to cheer her up a little, as I swirled my drink around, and listened to the ice clinking against the inside of the glass.

"I need to do something," said Janice. "Maybe I should try and get a gastric band?"

"No," said Ted. "Why would you maim yourself like that? Why would you have major bloody surgery when you're on a course that will help you lose it naturally, without some bloody surgeon sticking a knife in you?"

"Ted's right," I said. "I like Liz. I think she's going to be really good for us all."

"I didn't expect to like her much," said Ted. "Especially given the weird outfits she wears, but she's very good at identifying what the problem is and getting to the nub of it, and not letting you wallow in it. I think that's good."

"I don't think I'll ever be able to do it," said Janice. "I really don't. As I said last week, I started eating heavily when my mum died, and I can't sort out the eating without talking about my feelings around Mum's death, which I find difficult. I can't see that changing anytime soon. At least you managed to bring some humour into it, Mary, I just seem to be in floods of tears the whole time."

"Yes, but then she tells me that I'm using humour to hide my anxiety and feelings."

"I think we all do that a bit," said Ted. "I noticed you didn't want to dwell on what you thought had caused your eating problems."

"No."

"If you want to talk about it at any stage. You only have to call."

"OK," I said, but I knew there was no way I could talk about it. "I think it's great that we're all here for one another."

"Amen to that." Ted raised his pint and clinked my wine glass.

"I loved your story about the guy in the flat below seeing you shovelling chips into your mouth, while you were covered in grease," said Janice, with a smile. "That made me laugh a lot. Such bad timing that he came along. What did you say his name was?"

"David," said Ted.

Janice and I both looked at him, impressed that he was able to remember Dave's name.

"Yes, Dave," I said. "What a good memory you have, Ted."

Ted nodded. "So what's the story with this Dave then?"

"Nothing," I said. "I've had a few dalliances with him but always end up feeling horrible afterwards. He makes me leave before it's light so that no one sees me coming out of his flat...you know...things like that. All very horrible. I always think that if I was slim it would be different. He wouldn't be ashamed."

"He sounds like an absolute dick," said Ted. "Sorry if that's blunt, but – Christ – no one in the world should be ashamed of being seen with you. You're...well...you're lovely, Mary. He's just using you. Tell him to piss off...you deserve more than that. If he upsets you again I'll go and sit on him, that'll teach him."

"Thank you." I tried to think through the scenario of Ted turning up and sitting on Dave. "But I know he really likes me. I just need to lose weight and everything will be OK."

"I'm with Ted." Janice had returned from the bar with our second drink of the evening. This is the problem with being in a round. You can't go out for one drink, you have to have the number of drinks as there are people around the table.

"You are both really kind, but I know he really likes me. I just need to lose weight." I was aware I was repeating myself and that they both thought I was nuts.

"Nobody needs to lose weight for someone to love them," said Ted.

"Lose weight for yourself, for your children or for your future, but not because some dick with an over-inflated view of himself is embarrassed to be seen with you. Tell him to jog on, honestly."

"OK, OK," I said. "Let's leave it with the relationship advice. Janice, are you going to go and get extra help with looking back and understanding how you felt when your mum died, like Liz suggested? Or was that all a bit too much?"

Janice looked down at the table, clearly upset. "I don't know. The truth is that I don't want to think about it or talk about it, and the idea of digging through it and trying to understand it fills me with absolute horror. What do you think?"

"I don't know," I replied. "It's a difficult call. Some shrinks can be pushy, and force you to over-analyse and, kind of, make things worse. I don't know. Or perhaps that's only if you're a child. I'm sure they're fine really. Might be worth trying."

I saw Janice glance at Ted.

"Did you see a psychologist when you were younger, Mary?" she asked.

"We're talking about you, not me," I replied, as lightly as I could.

It was my turn to go to the bar, so I used the opportunity to escape from the unwelcome conversation. Despite the awkwardness of the last interaction, I was quite enjoying the evening. I could see the boxes of crisps sitting behind the bar staff, but didn't even feel moved to buy some.

Progress, surely?

3

THE THIRD SESSION AT FAT CLUB

*W*ell, there was good news and bad news to report before returning to Fat Club: I lost six pounds. I know! Huge achievement. I'd been really focused and thinking about the importance of eating healthily and exercising wherever I could. It was amazing.

The bad news... I slept with Dave. I know I shouldn't have, I know I should have tried and persuade him to make some sort of commitment to me before throwing myself under his duvet, but it doesn't work like that, does it? I thought if I spent a lot of time with him, and showed him it was enormous fun having me around, and how amazing I was in bed, he'd like me regardless of my weight.

I kind of thought he did. He said he did. Then at 5am his alarm went off, and he suggested I might like to leave because he was going to have to get into work early. He stood over me as I scrambled into my clothes, trying to arrange my hair and look as dignified as a woman possibly can while climbing into yesterday's knickers.

HE DIDN'T EVEN GIVE ME A KISS ON THE CHEEK. "I GUESS YOU'LL KNOW how to get home," he said as I scrambled out of the door, fussing and falling over the complicated locking system before spilling out onto the pavement with my shoes on the wrong feet.

I ambled up the steps to my front door, opened it and burst out crying. I cried quite a lot that day, and it was my day off work, so I had a lot of time on my hands in which to cry, which wasn't helpful. What also wasn't helpful was the fact that I saw Dave leave for work at 8am. He threw me out at five, but didn't leave till eight. It doesn't take a genius to work out what was happening there.

But the good news is, I didn't fall into a fried breakfast, or eat my bodyweight in crisp sandwiches. I didn't feel the need to fall into food when my mad emotions fell about me. For the first time. It might not sound like much of an achievement, but – honestly – it was one of the greatest achievements of my life.

I had quite a lot of communication from Ted and Janice through the week, we phoned each other regularly which was nice and, to be fair, knowing I had got those two on the end of the phone helped a lot with the fight not to eat rubbish all the time. I phoned Ted one night when I'd walked past the chip shop and really wanted to go in. "You need to tell me not to turn round and go back there," I said.

"Don't turn round and go back there," he said, in a very stern voice. "Give me your address and I'll come round now with an apple instead."

We both laughed at the ridiculousness of it all. Why did I have to ring someone and ask them to tell me not to go to the chip shop?

The lovely thing was that I didn't feel as if the battier part of me was being judged by Janice and Ted. My great friends at work, and my oldest friends – Sue and Charlie – were brilliant, but super slim and couldn't understand what I was going through. They didn't get it at all.

With Ted and Janice was like they were exactly the same as me. I think that's why this whole group therapy thing works. You stop feeling like a freak who is out of control and needs to just keep eating, and you start to feel like member of a community that understands you have a simple problem that can be easily sorted.

The only issue on which I continued to disagree with Ted and

Janice was Dave. Every time his name came up in conversation, Janice would sigh and Ted would bristle.

"Why would anyone treat another human being like that?" he'd ask. Then he'd add, "Actually, scrub that, why would any human being allow herself to be treated like that? That's what you need to ask yourself, young lady."

I knew he was right, but it didn't stop me hanging out of the window, watching Dave go to work, and trying to appear as alluring as possible on the steps of my flat as he returned, in the hope that he would invite me in again.

I arrived at the third session of Fat Club before Janice and Ted had turned up. Phil was sitting there on his own because his wife, and ever-present companion, had gone to the loo.

"Hello," I said as warmly as I could, but he just nodded and looked as if he wanted nothing on earth as much as he wanted me to leave him alone. When Philippa came back in, I retired graciously.

"Hello, trouble, where's Janice today?" said Ted, striding into the room and sitting next to me.

"No sign of her yet," I said.

"Janice said she was definitely coming," chipped in Liz, who was looking vibrant in a dress the colour of bananas. "I talked to her during the week and she was in good spirits."

"Oh good." Janice had seemed very depressed last week when we were sitting in the pub. I was glad she was coming. I felt very protective towards her.

"How are you doing? Good week?" I asked Ted.

"Pretty good," said Ted. "You probably noticed that I'm eight pounds lighter and looking very fly." He was relishing the small weight loss, as we all relished every development, however small, on the road to thinness. "I think I might leave the club now – my body is perfect," he added.

"Indeed," I said. "You don't want to lose any more, you might become anorexic, then you'll have to go to an entirely different support group."

"Yes, good point." He kissed me on the cheek. It was a lovely friendly gesture, but he went scarlet as soon as he'd done it. "Gosh, I'm so sorry," he said. "I didn't mean to do that."

Janice never turned up for the meeting which left me slightly anxious. I kept glancing at my phone to see if she had sent a text but there was nothing from her. As the time wore on, the silence from her started to really worry me.

In the end I sent her a note: "Oy, where are you? I can't do this fat girl stuff on my own, you know."

No reply.

The news from within the group was good – people were starting to feel more 'empowered' (sorry, such a horrible word) and were making decisions not to resort to eating all the time.

The meeting finished on a really positive note with lots of clapping and smiles and a huge grin of delight from Liz. In fact, the only thing missing from the whole evening was Janice.

"I can't get over how odd it is that she hasn't shown up," I told Liz, as Ted stood by my side, nodding to suggest that he agreed with me.

"I'll text Janice and tell her to meet us for a drink in our regular spot," he said.

"I wasn't thinking of going for a drink tonight, actually," I said. "I've got quite a lot that I need to do." I saw Ted's face fall.

It was a complete lie. I had nothing I needed to do. The reason I wanted to go home was to see whether I could bump into Dave. I was aware he came back from work at around this time on a Tuesday (I wasn't a stalker…just observant). I hadn't seen him since our drunken fumble and my early exit from his flat, and having lost a bit of weight, and feeling ever so slightly more confident, I thought it would be good to bump into him.

"Just one then." Ted took my arm and led me towards the Shipmate's Arms. I was too weak to refuse, so we sat in the corner of the pub exactly where we'd sat the last time. We had a really funny evening in the end, and I was glad I'd gone. We left a couple more messages for Janice, and Ted managed to calm me down a bit, reminding me that she was older, and probably had other commitments. It wasn't as easy for her to nip out to Fat Club. He was sure she was OK. He seemed convinced we would have heard from her if there was any problem.

The nice thing about being with Ted was that we were so similar… like brother and sister sometimes – exactly the same stupid sense of humour. There was something warm and reassuring about him. Always lovely and greatly entertaining.

When we left, Ted opened the door for me in a very gentlemanly fashion. He managed to tread that thin line between always treating me like an equal which I loved, while managing to do all the charming, gentlemanly stuff that made me feel special.

His behaviour was a reminder of how long it had been since any man had treated me properly. Men don't open doors for fat girls. Sorry, it might sound like a horrible thing to say, but when I was sweet and pretty and slim, men opened doors. Since I became fat they'd take one look at me bulldozing my way down the street and think 'well that one can clearly open the door herself – blimey she might take the whole thing off its hinges.'

I'm joking – sort of – but it's also true that men are more gentlemanly the more delicate and feminine you are, and 16 stone of fat is not considered remotely feminine to most men. The day you can't squeeze into your size 16 jeans is the day you learn to open doors for yourself.

4

THE VISIT

I was lounging in the bath when the call came through. It was Saturday morning and in traditional fashion I'd watched all the morning cookery programmes while salivating and fantasising about pies and cakes, and was now examining the rolls of fat banded around my waist and wishing I could lift them off to reveal a slimmer me underneath.

Ted's number popped up and I answered as cheerily as I could, trying not to splash and reveal that I was in the bath (something a little inappropriate about a man knowing you're wearing nothing but water and bubbles when he talks to you).

"Hello, fellow fatty, how you doing?"

"Not good," he said, and I sat up sharply.

"What's wrong? You sound dreadful." It was very unlike Ted to sound so downcast. He probably had just as many miserable days as the rest of us, but he always seemed to hide any angst and always be upbeat and cheery.

"It's Janice."

"Oh no, what happened?"

"I'm outside your apartment. I'd rather talk to you about it."

"Sure. How did you find out where I live?"

"Liz told me. Look, I'm sorry to disturb you, I wouldn't be here if it wasn't important."

"No, that's fine. Just give me a minute."

Rather than tell him I was in the bath, and that I would be 10 minutes, I jumped out of the bath water at top speed, and frantically dried myself while climbing into the plain pyjama bottoms lying on the floor. They could pass for casual trousers – it was fine. I'd been outside in worse. I teamed them with an over-large, long-sleeved t-shirt with a horrible, unflattering picture of Mickey Mouse on the front. It didn't make for an elegant look. If I'd known what information I was about to receive from Ted I might have rethought the decision to wear a novelty t-shirt.

Ted couldn't hide his surprise when I answered the door. He was used to seeing an extraordinarily large woman once a week when she was wrapped in a voluminous black coat. I suspect that seeing me braless and wet and wearing a t-shirt with a Disney character on it was altogether too much.

"Oh, have I disturbed you?" he asked, bending to look past me into the hallway, as if I might have men gathered there, just waiting for my attention.

"No, not at all. Just out of the bath, no problem. Come in."

As he walked through to the sitting room, I shouted, "I hope you don't mind mess." Most people say things like: "I hope you don't mind dogs." I'm forced to warn people about the utterly chaotic state in which I live. As I walked through, I grabbed the clothes scattered around the place and shoved them into a corner, wiping the table down with the sleeve of my t-shirt to make it look better.

I could see Ted looking at me with a gentle smile on his lips, either this was because he recognised my behaviour in himself, or he had never seen anything so ludicrous in his life. I was erring towards the latter.

I made coffee while Ted sat in silence – there were no chirpy asides about the horrendous state of the apartment, nor any mention of the biscuit barrel on the table.

"I put eight sugars in yours, I hope that's OK," I said when I returned with the drinks, but Ted wasn't listening.

"It's bad news," he said.

"No, I didn't really put eight sugars in – only joking."

"No, not the sugars, nutcase, the news I'm about to tell you."

I sat next to Ted on the sofa. Together we completely filled a settee which boldly claimed to be able to seat four.

"I called Janice on her mobile," said Ted. "And a guy answered."

"Ooooo...lucky Janice," I said.

"The guy was a nurse. Janice is in hospital."

"Oh no, is she OK?"

"Yes, she's fine now. She took an overdose."

Ted stopped for a while to allow this to sink in. "Mary, she tried to kill herself."

"Shit."

"Apparently she'd just had enough of it all... The catcalls, the 'oy fatty' every time she left the house. The fight to be dignified when squeezing into bus seats and the fact that no one wanted to sit next to her on the train."

I could feel the tears stinging in the backs of my eyes. We'd all been there, and I knew how upset it made Janice. Those of us struggling to control our weight have all been given the sort of abuse that would see the perpetrator locked up if they said it to someone black, disabled or mentally impaired.

"I can't believe she was feeling that low," I said, as Ted stared down at the brown and cream carpet on the floor under the coffee table. "She was miserable at Fat Club last week, but – Christ – not *that* miserable."

"We all seem OK on the outside," said Ted. "Don't we? I mean – that's what we do. We all seem *not that miserable*."

GOING TO HOSPITAL TO VISIT SOMEONE WHO TRIED TO KILL THEMSELVES because they couldn't stand being fat any more is not a pleasant thing for anyone to do. I'd suggest it's infinitely harder to do, and more emotionally crucifying when you yourself are morbidly obese. We asked which ward she was on, and I'm sure the nurse looked down at my stomach, and the way my t shirt rounded it.

Janice was sitting up in bed when we found her, and looked embarrassed when we walked up to her. "Gosh, you didn't have to come," she said, looking at me and then at Ted. "You must have a million things to do. You really didn't have to come out here and see me."

I wanted to reach out and hug her, to hold her close and tell her never, ever to hurt herself again. But I didn't. I'm too British for all that. I just reassured her, told her there was nowhere I'd rather be, and sat on the small wooden chair near the bed, handing her a bunch of flowers we had picked up on the way.

"How are you feeling?"

Her eyes filled with tears. "I feel much better, thank you for coming."

"Janice I'm so sorry, I don't know what to say. You should have rung one of us, or talked to us, perhaps we could have helped?"

"No one could've helped. I was too low to reach out to anyone," she replied.

"But, I wish you'd said something...anything. We could have tried to help."

"Mary you're lovely, and I really cherish your friendship, but there are some things that no one can help with."

"Just as long as you know we're here, and we care about you," said Ted. He leaned over and kissed Janice on the head in such a tender way that I felt my heart shift a little inside me. What good people they were. Really good people.

Since Ted had driven me to the hospital, he drove me back home, the mood having lifted considerably since confirmation that Janice was OK, she was out of danger and was going to be fine. She even talked about coming to the next Fat Club session. We'd both been shaken considerably by the realisation that she had got so low, and how desperate she'd felt. We vowed to make sure we talked to one another if we ever felt bad.

"Promise me you'll call," said Ted. "You know…if you ever feel really low."

"I promise I will," I replied. "Do you want to come in for coffee?" We had arrived at my flat. Ted nodded appreciatively.

"Or we could nip out for something to eat?" he said. "Let me buy you a late lunch, or early dinner. I haven't eaten…most unlike me."

"Neither have I," I lied, hoping he didn't remember the cookie jar on the coffee table and the plates discarded on the side in the kitchen.

"Then, after lunch, if you fancy it, we could go to a party later at a pub not far from here. It's just a leaving do for a friend who's moving away, but it'll be fun. Come with me. I'll drive, and I'll make sure you get home safely afterwards. Anyway, see how you feel after lunch."

"Sure." I wasn't at all sure about the drinks party but I definitely fancied lunch. "Let me go in and get changed quickly. I won't be long."

"You look absolutely fine like that," he said, as I struggled to open the door. I hadn't even tried to fasten the seat belt. Fat ladies and seat belts are a very unhappy combination.

"No, I have to get changed," I said. I'm not the most fashionable girl around, but even I would think it inappropriate to go out for lunch with a man while dressed in pyjama bottoms and a hideous t-shirt, while wearing no underwear at all. Even fat girls have standards, you know.

"No problem," said Ted.

I clambered out of the car, half stepping, half rolling my body out of the door. Ted followed me and the two of us waddled across the road. As I approached the little gate I saw Dave coming out of his flat. He looked like he was off to the gym. He was stubbly, unkempt and looked absolutely gorgeous. Dave glanced at me, at Ted, and back again.

"Hello, what have we got here then?" he said.

"This is Ted," I muttered, while Dave's handsome face looked at mine. "Ted's just a friend, you know. Just someone I met, not a boyfriend or anything. Just someone I know."

"Oh I see." Dave gave a smile. "Well then, Ted, you won't mind if I ask Mary whether she fancies coming round for pizza later. Perhaps to watch a film or something?"

"Sure, I'd love to." I didn't stop for even half a second to consider my words.

"Actually, we've got plans," said Ted. He was right, of course, we did have plans, but in that moment, rather shamefully, I just wanted him to go away.

"We'll do that another time," I said, my voice ringing with irritation. I couldn't look Ted in the eye. His shoulders were slouched over and his face was full of confusion. "You might as well head off now. I'll see you on Tuesday at the club, OK?"

"What club's that?" asked Dave.

"Fat Club," I responded.

"Ha ha, perfect," said Dave. "That's hysterical. The two tubbies from Fat Club."

Ted looked from me to Dave and back again, then he walked back out of the gate, across the road and got into his car. My insides felt crushed. What the hell had I done?

Dave watched Ted waddle away from us, smiling victoriously. "That's funny: Fat Club!" he said. "See you around 4pm, OK?"

"Looking forward to it," I said seductively, as I let myself into my flat. I knew I had treated Ted abysmally, but I had such a thing about Dave and I desperately wanted to spend the evening with him. I'd lost 10lb. Ten pounds! Dave needed to see my new body. Also, I convinced myself, I needed cheering up after the day I'd just endured. A lazy evening on Dave's sofa, with the prospect of a bit of physical action later was everything I needed. I did feel terrible about Ted though…really bad.

5

MY HOT DATE WITH DAVE

By the time 4pm arrived, I was dressed up in the best lingerie you can get in a size 42GG, and feeling good. It was a peculiar time to meet for pizza – it wasn't lunch and it wasn't dinner. Still, it was an invitation from Dave, so I wasn't going to question it or analyse it too closely.

I wandered down to his flat in my best black trousers which were now very loose around my waist. Yes! I could have put smaller ones on, but I decided to go for the bigger pair which were both smarter and gave me the lovely warm feeling of being loose, and thus reminding me of the weight I'd lost. I knocked on Dave's door; there was no reply. The lights were off inside and the flat gave the impression of being entirely empty. I waited for about 20 minutes (I know what you're thinking – who would wait for 20 minutes? Christ, woman, get a grip) and then went back upstairs, got a pen and paper and made a note which I pushed underneath his door. I was just retreating when Dave arrived back from the gym. He looked at me blankly.

"You told me to come down for pizza and video?" I said.

"Oh, OK then, yes – sure, you can you come in." He didn't sound overly excited about the prospect.

His flat was in a state of chaos, much like mine, but for some reason – perhaps because I'm female – I admonished him lightly and offered to help clear it up.

"Sure," he said with a smile, removing his t-shirt to display his quite spectacularly gorgeous torso.

"I'm going to have a quick shower, tidy if you want."

I'd meant that we could tidy up together in a kind of flirting foreplay sort of fashion. I wasn't offering to become his cleaner.

Still, I wanted to get into his good books, so while he showered, I started rounding up all the old packaging, cans and other assorted rubbish that had been thrown around the place. I shoved them into a bin bag. Dave was in his bedroom by now, presumably getting dressed.

"The Hoover is in the cupboard under the stairs," he said.

I knew it was ridiculous to get the Hoover out and clean his flat, but I was also madly happy to be there, and thought he would be so grateful, it would make everything good between us. I pulled out the Hoover and ran it round the flat, polishing the surfaces as I went, making it look lovely. Dave walked out with his jeans on...no shirt. Yes.

"You're an angel." He kissed me on the tip of my nose. "One other thing – you aren't any good at ironing, are you?"

"Um, I guess, why?"

"I have no shirts to wear."

I put up the ironing board and plugged in the iron and I know what you're thinking – you're thinking – this woman is a bloody moron. Well, yes, perhaps you're right. Dave stood there shirtless (a happy moment in the whole unedifying, desperate mess), and I ironed the shirt he handed to me, taking care to make sure it was perfect. Because somehow, somewhere, in the deep recesses of my soul I thought he might glance at himself and see how good he looked and feel great, and associate me with that feeling. It was a long shot, but my 'relationship' with Dishy Dave was built on long shots.

I handed him the still warm shirt and put away the ironing accoutrements.

"The flat looks great," he said. "Emma's coming round later, she'll be very impressed."

"Emma?"

I felt a dagger tear into my heart. Not that I thought he didn't have girlfriends, I knew damn well he had girlfriends – bloody dozens of them – but I thought tonight would just be about me, I also thought that seeing how I was getting slimmer and looking better, this would prompt him to dump all those other idiots, and the two of us would be together, forever.

"Do you mind if we don't get pizza?" he said. "I'm straight from the gym; I might just have a power shake or something."

"No, that's fine by me." It was fine – I didn't want to eat pizza. I'd said yes to pizza because I wanted us to spend the evening together. I fiddled with my hands in my lap and tried to think of something to say…something that would please him.

"I've lost some weight," I said, flinching as I heard the words and the way they rang with desperation.

"Well done," he said. "Where have you lost it from?"

"I mean – I've just lost weight generally, I've been going to this club, and I'm determined to lose loads of weight," I said.

"Of course…Fat Club." Dave collapsed with laughter. "Oh my God, that's hysterical," he said, wide-eyed with excitement. "You and that fat bloke from earlier. Just the funniest thing ever. Do they round up all the fatties and put them in one room to talk about food?"

I'd never seen him look so animated or laugh so much, so I joked along with him for a while, trying to smile and giggle at something that was actually quite serious. Then I thought about Janice and stopped abruptly. Then thoughts of Ted came into my mind; lovely, sweet, kind and funny Ted.

"God that must be hysterical," said Dave, falling into the recently plumped-up cushions on his sofa and laughing out loud. "Just a whole load of really fat people talking about why they can't stop eating. Honestly that must be so funny. Can you tape it for me?"

"Look, if you've got plans, I'll head off," I said.

"Why?" said Dave. "She is not coming for another hour... We can do that thing I like when you get your enormous titties out and I cum on them."

"I've got stuff on." I moved towards the door, and opened it, while he stayed on the sofa.

"Well, thanks for tidying up," he said, as I left, pulling the door behind me.

What the hell on earth was wrong with me? Why had I given up a lovely night with a genuinely decent, nice man, to go there and be humiliated by that moron? I let myself into my flat and called Ted's number, it rang out and then went to answer phone. He didn't want to talk to me, who could blame him?

Next I went onto Facebook, and I don't know why but I started looking for him on there. I found Ted's profile fairly easily, and smiled as I read his updates. He was really funny. Self-deprecating. Witty. Popular.

There were pictures of him as a sportsman and he looked bloody gorgeous...much better than Downstairs Dave has ever looked. Then pictures of him having his facial hair shaved into its current state. He'd done it for charity. Three of them had let children at a cancer hospital design their facial hair arrangements in order to raise money for charity. Oh God, I'd been mocking that daft facial hair but it was all for charity. He was such a nice guy.

Then it suddenly dawned on me how many female friends he had on there. All the comments after his jokes were from women...all telling him how wonderful he was and what fun he was. They all hoped to bump into him soon.

Bloody hell.

Shit.

He was kind and popular and obviously had female attention coming out of his ears.

There was a reference to a drinks party in a pub tonight. I wondered whether that was the one he'd asked me to go to with him? Bugger – it looked great. His friends had posted funny messages about how much they were looking forward to it, and daft pictures of the group altogether. The party looked like it would be brilliant. Ted was at the centre of all the pictures, being silly and having a laugh.

Bollocks. What an idiot I was.

I went into the kitchen and looked around. I took out two cream crackers and nibbled on them, absently, falling onto the sofa and flicking through Google on my phone as I did. I found lots of pictures of Ted as an aspiring rugby player and many articles about him.

Why hadn't I looked him up before? Presumably because I wasn't interested in him before. Now I was though. Quite suddenly I realised I really liked him and was overwhelmed by fascination. I had Google Fever. Nothing could stop me.

Saturday night TV was rubbish. I sat in front of a couple of game shows without really watching them – I was too intent on checking out pictures of Ted on my phone. Then the National Lottery results came on and I spent a lot of time imagining what I'd do if I won the millions. Perhaps I'd buy the whole house, and throw DD out from his flat below. I fantasised for quite a long time about him lying on the pavement, begging me to throw him crumbs.

Every so often I'd phone Ted but my calls all went unanswered. I'd cocked everything up.

Then, it occurred to me. Why didn't I go to the party?

Directions to get there were fairly simple, I just had to take two buses and I would be partying with Ted and his friends. Sod it, I was wearing my wonderful (if large) lacy lingerie, and my trousers were loose, what did I have to lose? I picked up my handbag, grabbed my lipstick and covered my lips in scarlet gunk.

As I stepped out of my door, I was greeted by someone who looked like they'd stepped off the pages of a magazine teetering into Dave's flat.

"Hi, are you Emma?" I asked. "Are you heading into Dave's place?"

"Yes," she said, with one of those high-pitched Marilyn Monroe style voices the men seem to find so appealing.

"I'd give it a few minutes," I said. "His husband has only just left. He asked me to tell you."

. . .

BARBIE DOLL LOOKED AT ME WITH EYES AS WIDE AS THEY WERE BLUE.

"He still wants to see you, but you should be aware that he's married to a man."

I headed off with a cheery wave, leaving the woman standing on the steps, wondering what on earth to do.

Ha. I felt strong, I felt powerful and I felt magnificent. Now all I had to do was get myself to Wimbledon. I was quite excited. In fact I was very excited, this was a lovely thing – there was a man there who genuinely liked me for me. He had never asked me to iron a shirt or clean his flat. He didn't seem to want anything from me other than my company.

As I thought about the fun times we'd had sitting at Fat Club, laughing our heads off, I started to feel more and more excited. He was a really nice man. Why hadn't I seen that before? What was I doing messing around with Dodgy Dave when I should've been with Super Ted? I changed buses and began getting even more excited. I'd be there in 15 minutes. I checked my makeup in a hand mirror, preening my eyebrows and playing with my hair while adding yet more lipstick, oblivious to the stares of interest from those gathered on seats around me. Nothing mattered but looking as good as I possibly could for Ted.

I stepped off the bus. There was the pub right in front of me. Ted would be in there and I would be joining him. I had butterflies. When was the last time I'd had butterflies? I couldn't remember the last time I'd felt so excited. My hands were sticky so I wiped them against my coat, walking towards the door and forcing myself to go inside.

I was so nervous.

I walked in and couldn't see Ted, or anyone I recognised from the pictures on Facebook. I walked up to the bar and ordered a large glass of white wine. I'd just sit and drink it calmly, looking around until I saw someone who looked familiar, then I'd stroll over and see whether I could see Ted. I hadn't yet worked out whether to pretend I was here having a drink and bumped into him, or confess I'd seen this on Facebook and wanted to come and see him. I guess I thought I might judge his reaction to my presence before revealing to him why I was there.

It was odd, but there was no large gathering of people in the pub. It was packed, all the tables and chairs were taken up, but no sign of a group that looked anything like a big group. I decided to call him again, but once again it went straight to answer phone.

This was becoming a bit of a nightmare, and I had no idea what to do.

"Excuse me," I said to the barman. "Are there any private parties here today?"

"Yes," he said, pointing to the far door. "Just go through there, up the stairs, push the door on your left and that's the function room, there's a party going on in there."

Ahhhhhh! That made sense. Finally I would get to see Ted.

"Thank you so much," I said, feeling those butterflies all over again. I stood up, downed the rest of my drink, and headed off. I went up the stairs and into the door on the left, and there was a party in full swing. Brilliant. This was it. All the people seemed about the right age. Still, it was quite odd walking into a party in full swing when you were on your own, especially when you hadn't been invited.

I tried to look as confident as possible and sat at the bar, ordering a drink. I went to my purse to find the money, but the barman stopped me. "It's a free bar," he said. That made me feel all the more awkward and embarrassed. I didn't want to steal drinks off these people; I just wanted to see Ted. Luckily, everyone had had such a good time at the free bar that they didn't seem to notice there was an intruder in their midst.

I sat and drank my drink, playing on my phone, pretending to text someone, laughing to myself and looking as if I was having a jolly good time at the strange party with these people I didn't know. I was fairly sure Ted wasn't in the room, but perhaps he was and I couldn't see him? Perhaps he was in the loo?

I had another drink, my awkwardness and embarrassment growing even further because this time I was ordering a drink when I *knew* it would be free. It was all too ridiculous, but to insist to the barman that I wanted to pay because I didn't know the person whose party it was, or indeed any of the guests at the party, would be more ridiculous still.

I took a walk around the circumference of the room as groups of drunk friends jostled and took pictures of the partygoers enjoying the night. One guy tried to grab me into a group shot, but I managed to wriggle away. Everyone was drunk and having a great time, pictures were being taken and jokes were being told. It was a lovely party, but Ted wasn't at it. I called his mobile again; no answer.

I had walked around the room three times, stared at everyone until they felt uncomfortable, and avoided about 20 photographs. It was time to go home.

6

THE FOURTH SESSION AT FAT CLUB

I was excited, but quite nervous, about seeing Ted at Fat Club. He had not responded to any of my calls, or replied to any of my texts so this felt like the only way to talk to him. I'd really pissed him off. I just wanted everything to be OK between us again. I wanted him back in my life.

Janice wasn't going this week so there was no chance of us having our Three Musketeers gathering in the pub afterwards. Perhaps just Ted and I could go? That would be nice. In tribute to that thought, I had dispensed with my usual big black, cover-everything coat, and wore a cherry red cardigan instead. I then put the black coat on top, of course, because I'm not an idiot.

I'd been in communication with Janice many times over the week and had met her for a coffee. She was feeling better all the time, and had started seeing a psychiatrist which she said was helping her a lot.

When we'd met, I'd sworn her to secrecy and told her that I really liked Ted. I hadn't realised how much I liked him at first, but now I did. I also told her about the night from hell when I'd traipsed all the way over to Wimbledon to see him.

Janice laughed at that bit. She loved the idea of me at the party, not knowing anyone, but pretending that I did. "My God, woman, you've cheered me up," she said.

"This is the sad bit," I said. "What part of this is cheering you up?"

In truth, though, it was so bloody farcical that it was funny.

"You sitting there, drinking free drinks," she said. "If I'd been well I would have come with you."

Ted was already at Fat Club when I walked in, but there were people sitting either side of him, so I couldn't get right next to him. Instead, I waved and smiled at him from my seat, and he just looked down at his notes. I'd tried to call him so many times and sent dozens of friendly texts, apologising. I'd left a message saying that I couldn't wait to see him on Tuesday night. He didn't reply to anything until this morning when he sent a simple one saying: "See you tonight." Not exactly a ringing endorsement of our friendship, but at least he was communicating with me.

The other thing I should tell you is that I'd lost some more weight, bringing my total weight lost to 14lbs. Fourteen pounds! Can you believe that? That's a stone, that is...a bloody stone!

"Come on, Mary," said Liz, running her hands through the new green streaks in her hair and pulling her pink cardigan around her. "Your turn to talk. Tell us how your week went."

Ted had spoken before me, and updated everyone on Janice, so I added that she sent her love and was feeling much better now. Everyone clapped and their murmurs of support filled the room.

"How has your week been apart from that?" asked Liz. "Tell us about your eating."

"OK. I'm managing not to shovel down lots of food, I've lost some weight and I feel much better. I'm genuinely feeling like I might be able to do it this time. You know, shift a load of weight and get myself healthier and fitter."

"That's wonderful news," said Liz. "And how is it all making you feel?"

"Good," I said, preparing to sit down.

"Sometimes when people have been using food as a crutch for a long time, they really feel the absence of it when it's taken away, and they need something else... Have you been drinking more? Walking more? Gambling, buying clothes or doing anything else in an obsessive way?" she asked. "Try to share everything so we can all really help one another."

"No, I'm OK," I said.

"Good. That's really great to hear. You haven't shared with the group quite as much as the others have about your reasons for overeating in the first place. You hinted, right at the beginning of the course, that something had happened to you when you were younger. If you decide that you want to talk about that, we're all here for you."

"Thanks. I'm OK, thanks," I said.

"Right, well let's end it there for this week," said Liz.

I turned around to talk to Ted, but he'd jumped up and headed out of the room. No goodbye. Not a word.

"Mary, if you want to talk, but don't necessarily want to share your feelings with the group you can always call me," she said. "Don't ever feel like you're alone, will you."

"No," I said, still watching the door that had slammed shut after Ted's hasty departure. "I won't. Thank you."

7. ONE WEEK LATER, SESSION FIVE OF FAT CLUB

"Hello, anyone there?" I was standing round by the bins, shouting up at the window. "Hello."

Silence. Not a whisper.

How odd. Luckily, I was in plenty of time for Fat Club. It didn't start for another half hour, so there was no panic, but it would be useful to get some sort of response. I wandered onto the street and looked up and down it, then sat on the wall and checked through my messages.

"Hi, it's me," I typed in. "I'm outside your flat – am shouting up at your window like some sort of loony but you can't hear me. Please come down soon before someone calls the police and they arrest me." I put a smiley face after the message, to indicate that I was only joking about the police coming, but I was very serious about wanting her to come out soon. This is the problem when someone you know has tried to harm herself…you're forever worried that she might do it again. Every time Janice hadn't replied to a text or not taken my call, I'd been thrown into a blind panic about where she was and what she was doing. Like now. Janice's house was in darkness in front of me, bar one lit window. I'd spent 15 minutes shouting up at that solitary light and there had been no response.

I rang the doorbell again, while simultaneously calling her. She knew I was coming to meet her so we could travel to Fat Club together. We'd spoken only this morning. Shit, what should I do if she didn't answer? Who should I call?

"Janice, it's me again. Look – no problem if you don't want to come tonight – no pressure at all. I just need to know you're OK. PLEASE send me a text to tell me that everything is alright x."

Nothing.

It was 10 minutes till Fat Club was due to start and 20 minutes after the time I had arranged to be at Janice's house. This was now odd. Bollocks. I couldn't sit there all evening and miss Fat Club – what would be the point of that? But I had to check that Janice was OK. I couldn't go anywhere until I'd heard from her.

Every part of me wanted to ring Ted. I knew he'd be able to help; he'd know what to do. But I also knew that the last thing he wanted was to get a call from me.

I banged on the door again, shouting up at the window, "Hi, Janice, it's me – Mary – I've come to walk to Fat Club with you. Are you there?" Nothing.

Perhaps if I texted Ted? That wouldn't be so awful, would it?

"Hi, I'm outside Janice's house. I arranged to meet her here 20 minutes ago but there's no sign of her. Not sure what to do..." I wrote.

He called straight away.

"Ted, I'm really worried," I said. "There's no sign of her, I've shouted and texted but no one's come to the door."

"OK, don't worry. I'm just pulling up outside the community centre; I'll come over there now. What's the address?"

I gave him the address and it took about a minute for his car to come screeching down the road. He jumped out, running towards me – a superhero in loose-fitting jogging bottoms.

"I just can't get any answer from her," I said.

Ted banged on the door in a very manly fashion, and eventually we heard a shout from a lady at the window above. "Will you just go away," she said in an old-sounding voice. I stepped back so I could see. She was, indeed, very elderly and looked quite scared.

"Is Janice there?" I said.

"No. There's no one called Janice here," she replied. "Stop screeching at my door, will you."

"Are you sure we're at the right place?" asked Ted.

"Yes." I opened my phone and looked at the text Janice sent with her address in it.

"Yes, this is it," I said triumphantly. "It says 10a Bath Avenue."

"No, this is Bath Road," said Ted. "We're in the wrong place, you numpty."

We waddled at high speed down the steps, jumped into Ted's car, and whizzed round to Bath Road. There – sure enough – standing outside 10a was Janice, her coat wrapped around her against the cold, looking slightly miffed.

"Sorry, sorry," I said, as we pulled to a halt next to her. "I went to the wrong address. I'm an idiot. But why haven't you got your phone turned on?"

"Oh shit." Janice looked at her phone and saw the messages I'd left and the calls I tried to make. "I left it on mute from when I was in the hospital earlier. Sorry."

"Hospital?" Ted and I cried, in unison, glancing at each other.

"Just a check-up, nothing to worry about," said Janice.

All three of us bombed down to the community centre, running through the doors 15 minutes after the class had started.

"I'm so sorry we're late," I said, as Liz's face lit up at the sight of us. "It's completely my fault."

"She doesn't know her avenues from her roads," said Ted.

I looked at him and smiled. Ted smiled back. YES!

It was a moving session in which Janice tried to explain to a group of overweight people why she'd tried to take her own life...without saying that it was because she was overweight. She talked about the misery and anger she'd felt and how she felt judged, rejected and horrible. Everyone smiled. She was preaching to the converted, but every one of us was wondering how she got so low. We'd all had moments of frustration, anger and despair. What had happened to Janice to make her think that death was an alternative to dieting?

Afterwards we headed for the pub. Janice was emotionally drained after speaking out about her attempted suicide so stayed quiet for most of the time. Ted seemed relaxed and happy as he downed his pint and flicked through some messages on his phone. It wasn't quite the same as it had been in the past – with Ted and me laughing and joking constantly – but it was a step in the right direction. At least we could get along together.

"Does it help to talk about it like that?" I asked Janice. "You know – share the details of it? I find it really, really hard to go into all the details about emotions and feelings. I'm happy to tell people about my food intake and my weight, but as soon as the questions start about how I felt, or what emotions it brought up, I clam up straight away."

"We've noticed." Janice touched my leg affectionately. "I agree with you – it's horrible to talk about it, and you feel very vulnerable and a bit silly at the time, but it does make you feel better afterwards."

"Good," I said. "I'm so glad you're feeling better."

I looked up and Ted was staring at me with narrowed eyes. "The weirdest thing," he said.

"What?" Janice and I chorused.

"It doesn't matter."

"What doesn't matter?"

"Nothing," he said. "Nothing, it's not important."

"I'm intrigued now," said Janice. "You have to tell us what's on your mind."

"Well, I was just scrolling through Facebook and some friends have put up pictures from a drinks party they had a couple of weeks ago. I didn't go to it, but there's a woman who seems to be kind of sneaking around in the background, but seems to be in every picture. My friends have all circled her and written 'Anyone know who this is?' And the odd thing is it looks exactly like you, Mary."

8. SESSION SIX, THE FINAL SESSION AT FAT CLUB

In total, over the six weeks that the Fat Club sessions had been running, I'd lost 19lbs. I was comfortably down a dress size, I felt better than ever and I'd met a man I really liked: that was the good news.

The less good news was that I still had about 60lbs to lose, and the man I liked was aware that I may have gate-crashed a party of all his friends that I wasn't invited to and had crept around in the background like some sort of lunatic.

I denied everything when Ted mentioned it last week, of course, despite the fact that Janice was sitting there and she knew it to be true.

"But it looks just like you," he'd said, while I tried to change the conversation by asking them both whether they liked my boots. It was only when I realised that the boots I was trying to distract them with were the same ones I was wearing in the picture that I took my foot off the table and downed my wine. "More drinks anyone?"

Eventually Ted let it go, though I could see him looking from my handbag to my coat and thinking 'the woman in the picture has exactly the same stuff as you...' He had every right to be confused but

I couldn't offer any sort of explanation that would reassure him about my sanity. So I'd just stayed silent.

That was last week, now we were back in our run-down community centre for the last session of what has been an amazing course. Everyone was there except for Liz. This was the first time that she hadn't been there before us, grinning warmly, while dressed in some peculiar outfit, and waiting to greet us all like toddlers on our first day at nursery.

"I'm sorry," she said, bowling in dressed in a canary yellow coat, clutching piles of literature and folders, looking windswept and unkempt. "I have so many bits of paper to give you and I just went and left them all at home. I had to turn back and the traffic was terrible. All OK now though. Right, how's everyone feeling?"

There were mutters of general happiness from people as Liz took off her coat to reveal a bright purple jumper, black trousers and pea green shoes. It was a fairly moderate outfit for her, but the shoe choice was remarkable to say the least.

"Let's go round the room one final time, and then I want to tell you about the next stage in the overeaters programme," said Liz. "Janice, let's start with you, if that's OK. I know we spoke a little bit during the week, but I'm sure everyone in the room is keen to find out how you're feeling."

"I'm fine, honestly – no one needs to worry," said Janice. "You've all been so incredibly kind and supportive... I can't tell you what a difference it's made. I – um – sorry, this is all very emotional for me to talk about, but I hit a real low point a few weeks ago... I don't know what happened to tip me over the edge, but I had this blinding moment when I just didn't want to be here. Now I look back and I can't quite understand what happened in my head. I don't recognise the person who was so low that she couldn't face the future.

"I made a promise to Liz that if anything like that ever happens again, I will talk to someone. Talk to you guys, to be honest, because what I've learned from all your kind messages and sympathetic calls is that I've met some friends for life on this course. I'm so grateful to you all."

Janice spoke about the psychological help she had been getting and how much she was benefitting from talking through her feelings, worries and concerns. "I know it sounds odd, this whole therapy thing... I mean – how can just talking about an issue make it better? In some ways you might think it would make things worse. Talking about things might make them bigger in your mind. But it's not like that. I genuinely feel as if the problems and the pressure they exert on me are lifted by talking them through. It's as if you're getting them out of your mind when you share them. And you know what it's like when you have negative thoughts left festering in your mind – they grow and distort and become like little monsters in there. The help you've all given me, coupled with the psychological help I've been getting have made me happier and more content than I've felt for years. Thanks so much, everyone."

There was an enormous round of applause when she finished. I stood up and started clapping above my head, but people looked at me as if I was nuts, so I sat back down again.

Veronica spoke next. I still wasn't sure about her, which was probably a bit mean of me because I didn't know her at all. I mean, she was probably lovely, but there was something unattractive about the way she seemed to want to talk about her modelling career all the time. I was a really good gymnast when I was younger...I mean – really good. I competed all over the world, but I wouldn't mention that every time I opened my mouth. Somehow it felt wrong, too self-indulgent to be appropriate. You don't stand up and tell everyone how great you were. This was Fat Club, for God's sake, we were all morbidly obese, did we need to hear about her life as a size six model?

"One of the things I find really hard is letting go of the fact that I used to be a model," she said, and I must admit I thought straight away 'here we go again, Veronica, do tell us all about your modelling career. We're all desperate to hear everything about it.' But she surprised me. "I'm not saying that being a model is important... Gosh, it's not like you're trying to find a cure for cancer, or help dying kids, but it's one of those professions that, because it affects you away from work, starts to seep into your life. If you work in a shop, once that shop's closed, you don't have to work in the shop – it's as simple and straightforward as that. If you want to go out and have a huge take-away and get drunk, it's not going to have any impact on your job at all. But if you're a model, you still have to live like a model. Even if the catwalk shows are weeks away and you're not earning a penny from the profession, you can't go out for dinner and stuff yourself. You can't do anything that's going to make your skin look bad, make you fat or make you in any way unattractive.

"I'd go on holiday and still be eating cotton wool instead of food and drinking loads of water, and panicking like mad about whether the sun would damage my skin, or the salt water affect my hair. If you're a model, you're a model every minute of every day, not just when the shop's open.

"Can you imagine what sort of pressure this creates? No one can live like that, which is why so many models go off the rails and end up taking tonnes of drugs or mainlining whisky to cope with the hunger and the pain. The truth is that you can't live a life when you're always on show and constantly being judged, without having something to lean on.

"Hardly ever eating and being permanently exhausted is a rubbish way to live.

"I coped with it all by binge eating, and because of this I developed bulimia. Not very good bulimia because I put on a load of weight, as you can see from the state of me, but bulimia nonetheless. I'd binge and binge, usually late at night when everyone else was asleep, then make myself sick and cry myself to sleep. Then I'd have a shower, eat half an apple and head back to the studio to do more modelling. It was rubbish and it affected me deeply and now I don't have any idea how to eat properly. I never really learned that. Food for me was always a comfort, a warm blanket to wrap around myself when the world felt nasty and cruel.

"I know I can be a bit stand-offish at times, and I don't find it that easy to socialise and meet new people, but it's been lovely to be here, and to meet everyone and to realise not only that I'm not alone, but that it's all going to be OK. Because that's how it feels, you know. It feels like it's all going to be OK. I know that with hard work I can get rid of the demons and I've got some brilliant new friends, so thank you everyone."

I applauded Veronica wildly when she finished, then it was my turn. I really wasn't sure what to say. I felt so drained after the last two talks. It had been so moving listening to them but I knew that I wasn't able to share my past with people in the same way. I decided, instead, to share my present and my future.

"These sessions have changed my life," I said. "I came here wanting to lose weight, and I have lost quite a lot, to be fair. I've gone down almost two dress sizes and feel about a million times better. But I have also gained more than I have lost. I've gained confidence, and I have realised that I'm not alone. There are other people struggling too, and they – that's you guys – are very inspiring. There are two people who I've become particularly friendly with – and that's Janice and Ted – and I'd like to thank them for their friendship.

"I'd also like to make a bit of a confession – we all make mistakes, as we go through life, and I've made a few recently. One massive one. A guy I really like – let's call him, um, Tarzan – asked me out and I said yes, then another guy, a rather vain and idiotic guy – let's call him 'the wanker' – suggested I meet up with him on the same night.

"For reasons I can't possibly explain, I changed my plans and went out with the wanker instead, and I dumped Tarzan. Can you imagine anything more ridiculous? Dumping Tarzan and going out with a wanker?

"Anyway, so I went out with the wanker, and realised he was just using me, and I was bonkers, and really liked the first guy – Tarzan. So I rushed out of the wanker's house and I tried calling Tarzan loads and loads, but he didn't return my calls. I even went out that evening to the party he was supposed to be at, but he wasn't there, and all his friends were looking at me and trying to work out what on earth I was doing there."

I looked over at Ted and saw him smile as he realised that it had been me in those photos – skulking around at the back of the drinks party.

"Anyway, I don't know why I'm telling you all this," I continued. "I just want you to know that a kind and lovely, genuinely nice guy is better than an arsehole in a nice suit."

I sat down to confused looks and half-claps. No one really knew who Tarzan was. Liz was nodding, but I could see that she had no idea why I'd shared my bizarre dating story with the group either. Ted was looking down at the floor. I might never see him again, but at least he knew the truth – that I liked him and deeply regretted behaving the way I had.

Liz handed out lots of information for us to keep, including the details about the next stage – a 12-week course, starting in two months.

I would definitely go, I thought, as I gathered my things together and gave Janice a big hug. It turned out Janice was going as well, so that was good – at least I'd know someone. I said goodbye to everyone and went to the coat stand to collect my coat. Ted was standing there.

"You OK, Jane?" he said.

"Jane? No, I'm Mary."

"Oh for God's sake, woman. Me – Tarzan; you – Jane."

There was a gasp of understanding from all the others in the group. Now they knew why I'd told the story. "Oh, yes, I'm fine." I felt my cheeks scorch and turn an unflattering shade of scarlet.

"If that nickname sticks, I'll never forgive you," said Ted, giving me a little hug that told me everything would be OK. "Look, I have to go away for a few days for work. Do you fancy catching up when I get back? We could go out to dinner or for a drink or something?"

"I'd love that," I said.

"Good." He winked at me and made my insides somersault with joy.

Ted left and I looked round the room. Veronica was smiling at me.

"He's lovely; you two make a fab couple," she said.

"I know. I'm so excited. We're going to go for a drink when he's back. Is that – like – a date, do you think?"

"God, yes," said Veronica. "You have got yourself a date, young lady. What are you going to wear?"

"I don't know. I might buy something new. I haven't been shopping for ages," I said. "I might buy a new dress. What do you think?"

"I think you should definitely do that," said Veronica. "Why don't I come with you? It would be a great chance to get to know one another better, and I do know a bit about fashion and what looks good after all those years of modelling. What do you think?"

"I'd love that."

"Just text me, OK. Let me know when you're free and we'll meet up and get you the most knockout dress imaginable," said Veronica, as we headed towards the exit. "We'll make it a fun day with wine as well as shopping."

"Fab."

I hadn't felt so happy for years.

BOOK TWO

Adventures of an Adorable Fat Girl

1. WILL ANYONE EVER MAKE A FASHIONABLE, FLATTERING DRESS THAT FITS ME?

There is nothing on earth quite like the terror felt by a large woman in a compact changing room trapped inside a small dress.

And, today, ladies and gentlemen, that large woman was me. I don't know quite how it happened; one minute I was inching my way into a lacy, black skater dress; the next I was reeling in terror, unable to extricate myself from it.

The dress was too tight, there was no doubt about that, but I was convinced that if I just pushed a little more, everything would be fine and it would all fall into place. So I pushed...and wriggled...and ended up so far into the damn dress that every time I moved I felt the material stretch threateningly as if it might tear completely. The whole thing was bursting at the seams.

"Everything is OK?" came a voice from outside the cubicle. It was the skinny, dark-haired assistant.

I froze in terror.

"All fine." But that was a lie... I wasn't fine. I was well and truly stuck.

The woman outside must have known I wasn't fine; she was bound to have heard the huffing and puffing I was making a few minutes ago, along with the wheezing and groaning as I shrugged and wriggled.

"You manage to get on?" she asked in a soft Spanish accent.

I put my foot against the door.

"Yes, all fine. I've got the dress on."

And, to be fair, that was the truth – I had got the damn thing on. I had managed to squeeze it over my vast bosom and had forced my big arms into the lace sleeves. What was proving much more difficult was getting it off.

I looked at myself in the mirror; I looked like an overstuffed black-pudding.

I tried pulling at the sleeves but they wouldn't budge at all. They were made of lace so I was terrified to pull too hard in case the whole thing disintegrated in front of me. I tried lifting the dress over my head but the bodice part of the skater dress was staying tight on my body and the zip was stuck fast.

I called out to my friend Veronica, hovering outside the door waiting to see me emerge, looking delicious and gorgeous in a little black dress.

"Veronica, get in here quickly, I'm stuck."

"What do you mean 'you're stuck'?"

Veronica walked in.

"Oh, you're stuck." She smirked, then saw my beetroot red face and flustered disposition and thought better than to laugh at my predicament.

"This stupid dress is way too small, and it won't come off," I said. "It's a complete nightmare."

"They have a really odd sizing policy here," said Veronica support-ively. "Even really skinny girls find the clothes small. It's not your fault."

In truth, I suspected they had a perfectly reasonable sizing policy. It was my eating policy that was all wrong.

She suggested that the only way to remove the dress was from the bottom up, so she lifted the skirt of the dress to try and get it over my head.

"It won't go," I warned her. She pulled so hard that I feared she might take half my internal organs with her.

Still, the dress wouldn't budge. Veronica continued to pull, baring her teeth she yanked at the material with all her might and I pushed back with all mine.

"Try taking the dress from the arms," I suggested. "But be careful with the lace."

Veronica moved her hands to the sleeves and tried pulling from there. This had to work, surely. I pulled back as before, and with hindsight what happened next was probably inevitable, but I didn't see it coming. There was an almighty ripping sound. The pressure around my body disappeared and I felt free. The dress was off – that was the good news. The rather worse news was that the arm of the dress had almost detached itself from the bodice. On closer inspection I saw that the bodice itself was also ripped, and the zip was hanging off.

"Oh good God, no," said Veronica as we both stared helplessly at the damaged dress.

"What should I do?"

Veronica didn't answer me, so for some considerable time we both simply stared at the dress as if we might mend it by power of concentration.

"Get dressed," said Veronica, leaving the changing room with the badly ripped dress.

Once she was gone, I clambered into my capri trousers and powder pink A-line top, relieved to be in clothes that fitted. There were welts in my skin where the tight bodice of the dress had dug in around my waist.

I checked myself in the mirror, running my hands through my blonde hair.

God, I'm so fat. I hate that I look like this.

Like anyone of large size, I'd tried every diet imaginable. The only thing that ever worked for me was Overeaters Anonymous. I'd been on their six-week introductory course a few weeks earlier, and felt great afterwards. I'd lost weight and felt powerful for the first time ever. That was also where I met my awesome boyfriend, Ted, who was the love of my life. We'd both lost two stone each. It was also where I met Veronica and loads of other friends. I suppose you could say it changed my life. The second stage of the course was going to start in three weeks and I couldn't bloody wait for it.

I walked out of the changing room to see Veronica standing there.

"Where's the dress?" I asked. I knew I'd have to pay for it, I just wanted to get it over with.

"I gave it to the assistant and explained that it didn't fit," she replied. "Let's go."

"I have to pay," I said, but Veronica wasn't having any of it.

"Follow me," she said.

"But I feel terrible," I said. "I ripped the dress. I should've told them."

"The dress was too small."

"No, let's be honest about this: I was too big."

"Don't worry, this sort of thing happens all the time. They won't mind one bit. Let's go and meet the girls."

Veronica took my arm in a pally fashion and led me to the coffee shop down the road where we were meeting two of the other women who were on the first Fat Club course with us. I hadn't seen them since the course ended so was dying to catch up with them.

We marched along, with Veronica chatting happily and pointing out lovely clothes in lovely shops as we went, while I spent all the time envisaging a life behind bars. I kept thinking that the woman from Zara was behind us. Every time I saw a woman in black I thought she was following me and would arrest me and I'd be locked away from everyone I know. And what about Ted? I'd spent a lifetime trying to find a decent boyfriend, I couldn't lose him now.

"I need to go back and buy that dress," I declared.

Veronica looked over at me. "What dress?"

"The one I tried on and ripped. I need to buy it."

"Whaat? No you don't. Why would you buy a ripped dress that never fit you?"

"Because I don't want to spend the rest of my life behind bars."

"You're not going to end up behind bars. What are you talking about? I used to work in a shop, that sort of thing happened all the time."

"Did it? That makes me feel better."

In the coffee shop, Liz and Janice were tucked away in the corner, chatting and laughing so much that they didn't see us arrive. We ordered coffee and joined them, sliding onto the long, leather bench as Liz licked the foam from her coffee off the back of her spoon.

"You're here." Liz dropped the spoon with a clatter and wrapped me in a warm embrace. "It's so lovely to see you."

"You look great." Janice reached over to hug me.

Veronica put our coffees down on the table and was enveloped in the same affection.

"I'm dying to hear how you've got on since we last saw you," said Liz. "You both look very trim."

Liz was our leader on the Fat Club course, she wasn't 'fat', as such, but would certainly be described as 'sturdy'. Apparently she used to be huge and had worked really hard to get her weight down.

Janice was in Fat Club with Veronica and me and was one of my best friends there – she, Ted and I would sneak off to the pub after every session.

"Have you lost some more weight?" asked Janice which I was delighted about. I told her that I'd lost four or five pounds.

"Brilliant news on the weight loss, but you know what we all really want to know, don't you?" Liz winked at me. "We want to know if you're going out with Ted."

"Ah...Ted," I said, with a smile. "You want to know about Ted? I am totally in love with Ted. It all worked out...we're together and really, really happy."

Janice burst into applause, accompanied by Liz, and totally out of character, by Veronica.

"I'm so pleased, Mary," said Liz. "You two were so obviously meant to be together, I'm really happy that it's all worked out for you. Where is he now?"

"Amsterdam," I said. "He's in bloody Amsterdam."

"What's he gone there for?" asked Liz.

I knew what she was thinking… All those prostitutes and drugs… Not the ideal place for your boyfriend to be.

"His company is trying to win a big contract in Amsterdam, Ted has gone over there to meet the managing director of the company." I added (defensively): "He showed me all the paperwork and everything. He's so clever, if he pulls this deal off, it'll bring in millions to the company, and he'll definitely get a bonus and pay rise. It's amazing."

"When is he back?" asked Liz.

"He's back at Heathrow tomorrow night." I gave a small squeal of excitement that made Veronica turn and look at me sharply.

"I'm excited," I said, trying to explain the mouse-like squeak. "I haven't drunk a drop of alcohol since he left, I have been really good with my diet, and trying to walk as much as possible. I want to look super gorgeous for him when he gets back from his trip tomorrow… like Audrey Hepburn or something."

"Audrey Hepburn?" queried Veronica.

"OK, maybe more Marilyn Monroe or Diana Dors."

Veronica looked at me sideways. She could be horrible sometimes.

"OK, Diana Dors' big fat older sister."

"Don't be ridiculous," said Janice. "You're a beautiful, sexy, gorgeous woman. You look exactly like Marilyn Monroe. Ted must be delighted to have you by his side."

"Thank you," I said. "I just tried to buy a new dress to wear but it all went wrong. The worst, most embarrassing thing happened."

"What?"

"I went into Zara to buy a dress, but ripped it to shreds instead."

They both looked at me askance.

"Why did you do that?" asked Liz, stirring sweetener into her coffee. Not sugar. None of us would dare touch sugar in public. It would be worse than snorting cocaine in public, or defecating on the table.

"I didn't do it on purpose," I reassured them. "I tried on this beautiful dress but it was a bit tight and once it was on I couldn't get it off."

There were sympathetic 'oooos' from around the table. They'd all been there.

"Veronica helped me. She pulled and pulled and the thing ripped."

"Ahhh," said Janice. "Done that!"

"Have you?" I asked. "I felt awful. I wanted to go back and confess and offer to buy the dress. I felt like a complete criminal just leaving it there, but Veronica told me about the time she worked in a clothes shop and everyone did things like that."

"When did you used to work in a shop?" asked Janice.

"I've never worked in a shop. But madam here needed a bit of reassuring, so I pretended that I did."

"You never worked in a shop?" Oh God, this wasn't good. I should have listened to my own instincts and just bought the goddamned dress. "I'm going back."

They all looked at me as I jumped up. I didn't mean to cause a drama. I didn't want to storm out of the coffee shop. I just wanted to stop worrying about the damage I'd caused. "I'll be back in about five minutes," I said.

"Don't be so silly," said Veronica, but it was too late. I was already on my way back there to tell an undersized, gorgeous Spanish girl who didn't appear to speak very much English that the fat woman she'd been concerned about had been unable to get into the black dress with the lace sleeves and had ripped it and therefore now wished to buy it.

What I didn't realise was that as I left the coffee shop, the girls followed me. One fat lady marching down the street heading for Zara, with three fat ladies waddling along behind. I guess there was a funny side to it. The security guy on the door certainly looked twice. He probably thought I'd multiplied.

"Hi," I said to the assistant standing by the changing rooms. It was the same woman who had enquired after my well-being earlier. She smiled in recognition, but looked a little worried. She knew that nothing in this shop would fit me.

"Could I take this dress please?" I indicated my dress on the rail.

She reached over and took it off, seeing straight away that it was ripped.

"Is no good," she said. "Is rip here. No good."

"Yes, it's good. I want to take it with the rip," I said, trying to take it out of her hands.

"No, no. Is rip," she said, slowly, thinking that her accent was the problem. She showed me the way the sleeve hung off. "Is no good."

"Yes, it's fine. I want it."

"You want no good, ripped dress?"

"Yes, I want no good, ripped dress," I confirmed. I could see she thought I was completely mad. I could also see that she had seen my friends collecting behind me, like some sort of fat army in pursuit of a broken dress.

The commotion had come to the attention of the shop manager who wandered along, dressed head-to-toe in black of course, olive skinned, of course, big brown eyes, of course. Another living example of perfect Spanish beauty.

"Is problem?" said the manager.

"No problem," I said, pointing to the dress. "I want that dress."

The lady who had been serving me explained to the manager that the dress was ripped and that was why she wouldn't give it to me.

"Ahhh," said the manageress, understanding. She turned to me. "Is ripped." She spoke in the clearest voice she could muster. "No good. Ripped."

"I know," I replied. "I'd like to buy the ripped dress."

"No possible," said the manageress. "This is rubbish now. I take it."

"I would like to buy the ripped dress," I tried, aware that any sane shopper visiting Zara that sunny afternoon would have thought I was losing my mind. "Me want ripped and broken dress. I broke the dress. I need to buy it."

"No," said the assistant, looking at me ever-so kindly. "We can order you this dress, all new, not broken."

"Come on." Veronica pulled me away. "Let's go. This Zara experiment has failed."

One by one we trooped out of the shop, watched every inch of the way by two very lovely, and very confused, Spanish ladies, clutching a ripped, black skater dress.

2. ARTISTIC ENDEAVOURS

*W*e stood on the street looking at one another, neither of us quite sure what to say.

"Where shall we go?" asked Veronica.

Liz and Janice looked too shell-shocked by what they had just witnessed to be able to think of anywhere sensible to suggest.

Next to us was a small crowd, waiting to go into a white building with a large black door. The mixture of people in the queue was intriguing. Incredibly well-dressed men and women, and then what looked like a hen party of girls about my age – in their early thirties – giggling with excitement as they watched, waiting for the black door to open.

"It's going to open in less than a minute!" declared one of them.

We all stood, suddenly transfixed by the door and what it might reveal.

"Here we go," shouted another of the hen party women. "It's opening."

A man emerged wearing a jacket, black tie and white gloves. He bowed graciously and signalled for the three people at the front to go in.

"Isn't that Ashley Saunders?" I asked.

"Who?" said Veronica.

"The guy who does the travel on BBC Breakfast. You know him… always smiling and dressed in ludicrously bright coloured jackets. He's right at the front, wearing a blazer."

Veronica stared vacantly at the back of the man who delivered the news about the London traffic in the morning while Janice and Liz watched his glamorous older companion, bedecked in fur.

"I want to look like that when I'm older," said Liz.

"I wouldn't mind looking like that now," I offered. "At least she'd be able to get into the goddamned clothes in Zara."

"Are you ever going to shut up about that?" asked Veronica.

The group of younger girls was ushered through and we watched them giggle as they rushed through the door, thrilled to be granted entry into the inner sanctum.

"Come on, you come too, bring your friends," said the doorman. He was signalling to us, clearly thinking we were with the party that had just gone in.

"Come on," I said to the others. "Let's give it a try. What's the worst thing that can happen?"

Veronica gave me a stern look, but I couldn't be stopped.

"Follow me," I urged, strutting through the door.

Inside was a beautiful room with fabulous artwork all over the walls. Waiters wandered around, handing out glasses of champagne while others offered small, beautifully crafted canapés. They looked like pastry macramé. A string quartet played in the corner. It was the loveliest room I'd ever been in. A sudden wave of longing hit me and I wished like anything that Ted was standing next to me.

I wished he were right by my side, smiling down at me and gently putting his arm round me and hugging me close to him.

The four of us took a glass of champagne each, clinked our glasses together, and wandered to the side of the room to take a look at the paintings adorning the walls. Some of them were beautiful – spectacular blasts of colour and wonderful images. Others looked like they'd been done by a blind man using only his feet.

"It's so beautiful in here," said Liz. "And all the free champagne we want. How did we get invited?"

"Because we're fabulous." I winked at Liz. She smiled and regarded me with new respect, as we continued to marvel at the beautiful works of art and the immaculately dressed people wandering around, and drinking the free champagne.

"Thank you very much," I said, taking another glass and downing the whole lot in one. I was so thirsty. I know it wasn't terribly advisable to drink champagne to quench my thirst, but it seemed to be the only beverage on offer.

"Hi, yes, thank you." Another glass of champagne.

I would stop after this one. I just needed a couple of glasses to take the edge of the embarrassment of the ripped dress fiasco, then I'd rein myself in so I could look as good as possible tomorrow.

It seemed to us, as we walked around the gallery, that the pictures nearest to the door were the more 'arty' ones. You know – they actually looked like someone painted something that exists in the world. Really lovely portraits and pictures of scenes. Further into the room sat the more modern art – piles of discarded junk with enormous price tags on them. We wandered round looking at them, but no one was wildly impressed. Perhaps they were clever, but they weren't interesting, challenging or beautiful.

"Oh, thank you, yes please." Another glass of champagne. I'd stop after this one.

Liz, Veronica and I stuck together as we walked around, trying to look as if we knew what we were talking about, while Janice wandered off deep into the gallery.

Suddenly there was a clinking of a glass, and everyone gathered towards the centre of the room where a small podium had been erected. A man in black tie stood up to it.

"Ladies and gentlemen, welcome to the Northcote Art Gallery auction. I hope you have received your brochures and have had the chance to look at all the art on sale today. We will be starting with painting one…"

And so began an auction of all the paintings, sketches and weird installations that we had been examining. I know what I'm like, so I stepped right back out of harm's way, away from the throng, so they couldn't think I was putting my hand up. I wanted to be nowhere near the people who were indicating to the auctioneer that they had £40,000 to spend on a collection of twisted up coat hangers.

I had another glass of champagne, thinking I should really stop after that one.

"Come on," said Veronica. "Let's go for a wander and find Janice."

I could see by the glassy look in Veronica's eyes and the half-smile on her lips that she'd had way too much champagne. It was probably best that we moved away from the auction. We found Janice in the back of the gallery, where the daft modern art had ended, and there was a collection of more interesting pictures on the wall.

"I like this," I observed to Veronica. "Proper art."

There was a picture by Picasso, and an odd sketch of a giraffe by Salvador Dali – mad, but really quite fun and appealing. There were also line drawings and colourful landscapes – all by artists that I'd actually heard of.

"Are these not part of the main auction?" I asked.

"This is the silent auction," said an elegant lady in black. She was stick thin. The sort of woman who would never have imagined it was possible not to fit into the biggest dress in Zara.

"Is that different from the auction out there?" I said.

"Yes, that's the public auction. Here you write down your bid and the person who writes the largest amount wins the lot."

"Oh, that sounds fun," I said. "How much has been bid so far?" I'd seen the extraordinary amounts that had been bid in the public auction, I imagined these drawings would attract millions.

"Nothing yet. They will all be along when the public auction has finished."

Veronica and I looked at the clean sheets beneath the pictures. The minimum you could bid was £5,000.

"That seems really cheap," I commented. Some of the pictures around the corner had gone for hundreds of thousands.

"Oh, they won't go for £5k, it's just the minimum you can bid.

There would be no point in bidding at that level – the financiers in there will just outbid you later."

The lady with the champagne came back again, so I finished my glass, put it onto her tray and took another one. This was the last one. Definitely the last one. Everyone was looking blurred and the art was all starting to look like it was coming off the walls.

"You know what we should do," I said to Veronica in a half-whisper. "We should bid, so we can say we bid on Picassos."

"But we can't afford £5,000," replied Veronica, quite reasonably.

"I know! We won't get them for £5,000, but at least we can tell everyone we bid. We can take a photo of the bid. It'll be so funny. Come on, come on."

This was the greatest idea ever. We put down our glasses of champagne and signed our names, placing our bets, safe in the knowledge that we would never win these works of art. It was just so funny, and the champagne was so nice. And Veronica put the picture on Facebook and everyone was commenting. We laughed a lot. Then we had more champagne, then finally, finally, we decided it was time to go home.

3. BATTERED AND BRUISED

Oh Good God Alive, why do I do this to myself? Why? I clambered out of bed while a dozen men, armed with drums and drills danced and fought in my skull. I held onto the sides of my head, worried that it would split in two. All I had to do now was find a clock.

The kitchen. There was a clock in the… Shit, shit, shit, shit, shit. It was 9.15am. Bloody hell. I was supposed to get up at 7am, to be in work by 8am, but I didn't set my alarm. Of course I didn't.

I rushed to the bathroom, not letting my hands drop from the sides of my head. On the wall in the hallway there was a notice board with my LFBTTTCB campaign notes. If you're wondering what that collection of letters stands for, it's: Look Fabulous By The Time Ted Comes Back. Not catchy, but it worked. Except for the morning when it didn't work at all – the very day he came back, when I woke up two hours late, feeling like shit.

I couldn't work out what to do. I went to the loo, brushed my teeth and sat down heavily on the edge of the bath. Everything was hurting too much for me to think properly.

On my phone there were lots of messages. One from Veronica in which she appeared to be singing, or she was being attacked and was shrieking to frighten her attackers off. It wasn't clear which.

Then there was the predictable message from work in which my sarcastic and downright miserable boss was explaining the importance of punctuality and how vital it was to call in and explain if you were going to be off. "I'm trying to run a business, Mary," he said, like I didn't know. "Please behave professionally."

Christ. I had to call in straight away. I picked up the phone and dialled the number, hoping that some excuse for why I was late would come to me before he answered.

"I had a dentist's appointment," I said. "Sorry I forgot to tell you."

"You need to have dentist's appointments in your own time," he replied firmly.

"I would have, but this was at hospital," I replied. I felt very hungover and very sick.

"At hospital? Why, what were you having done?"

And that was where it started... I invented a tale about having a back tooth removed because of an abscess in the side of my cheek and I heard him go quiet.

"It's very swollen," I said.

"I'm sorry to hear that. You should have told me," he said.

"I'll be in as soon as I can get there."

"Are you sure you're OK to come in today?"

"Yes, I'll be fine. I'm just waiting to get checked over by the nurse and then I'll be there."

"You're still in hospital?" He sounded worried and I felt very guilty.

"Yes, but I'm fine, honestly."

"OK, but don't come in unless you're sure."

I had a quick shower and dressed in my lurid green uniform that made me look like Kermit the Frog, then I rushed out of the door, forgetting my hat (yes – we had to wear green and white stripy hats because the uniforms on their own didn't make us look stupid enough). I pinned the hat to my hair and piled back out of the door, straight into Dave, the bloody gorgeous guy from the flat downstairs.

"Looking good," he said.

"Yeah right," I replied, curtseying before dashing off for the bus stop.

"You can come down tonight wearing nothing but that hat if you like," he said.

I didn't stop to reply. There was a time, not too long ago, when I'd have been down there, wearing nothing but the hat before he could finish his sentence. No longer. I had a boyfriend, and if you hadn't realised this already – I was very fond of him.

IT WAS 10AM BY THE TIME I GOT INTO WORK, BUT EVERYONE WAS TOO concerned about my awful dental treatment to give me much grief. They'd heard the story of abscesses and hospitals and, frankly, they were amazed to find me still alive.

"My aunt had that, it was horrific. She was off for two weeks," said Ned, the young gardener who'd joined us after the last mass redundancy programme. He was young and cheap so perfect for Fosters DIY & Garden Centre. He was also lovely.

"My aunt's face was swollen and all blue," he added, and I realised that I hadn't faked any of the swelling or discolouration that would surely accompany major dental surgery.

I was called in to see Keith, my boss, who was apparently very worried about me. I wished I hadn't lied. I wished I hadn't drunk so much and been such a horrible mess last night.

BEFORE FACING KEITH I WENT INTO THE LADIES AND LOOKED AT MYSELF in the mirror. I didn't look wonderful, but I didn't look as if I'd had an operation of any kind. I took a wad of hand towels from the dispenser and soaked them in water, wringing them out then moulding them into the side of my mouth to create a lump. I didn't have any blue eye shadow on me but I did have a blue mascara, so I stroked it against the back of my hand, added a little moisturiser and wiped the resulting blue crème across my cheek to create a bruise-coloured sheen. I dabbled on some pink blusher and – I swear to you – it looked bloody realistic. The paper in my cheek pushed up towards my eye, leaving that half-closed. I looked like I'd undergone some emergency operation in my mouth. It was perfect. I was a genius. I should be working in the makeup department on *Casualty*.

I left the toilets and headed to Keith's small office at the back of the centre, right next to the cafe which always smelled soooo good. I ignored the smell of bacon and had a quiet smile to myself as I remembered that I hadn't eaten anything last night, and hadn't eaten this morning.

"God, Mary, you look bloody awful," he said when he saw me. "What the hell have they done to you?"

I couldn't talk terribly well with the paper in my mouth, and I didn't want to attempt to talk with too much animation in case I dislodged the fake swollen cheek, so I just stood there and nodded at him.

"Oh my God, your hand. Why's that so badly bruised?"

I looked down at the back of my hand. It was bright blue – like the sea when you go on holiday to Greece, like the sky on a summer's day. Not like the colour a hand should be at all.

"Is it bruised from where they put in the needle?" he asked kindly. He looked so concerned that I felt more guilty than ever. I almost wished I'd had a terrible mouth-related incident to justify such attention. I nodded at the needle question and he shook his head.

"If you had a general anaesthetic this morning, you really should be taking it easier. Why don't you work inside today, just keep an eye on the plants in the greenhouse and head off early if you need to."

I nodded.

Oh God, I was such a fraud. I really hated lying. Hated it.

As I walked out from the meeting with Keith, my mobile rang in my pocket. I had no idea what to do. I couldn't answer it with Keith watching because I'd just given an Oscar-winning performance of a woman who couldn't speak. I pulled it out and looked at it. I didn't recognise the number.

Keith strode out of his office and to my rescue.

"Shall I get that for you?" he asked, taking the phone and

answering in a brisk voice: "Mary's phone. How can I help you?" The caller spoke, and Keith's eyebrows raised.

"No, Right. Yes. Of course, I'll tell her. Yes. Indeed. I'm sure she'll be delighted. Of course. Yes. Thank very much for calling."

Then he handed me the phone with a quizzical look on his face. "You've just won a secret auction," he said. "A Dali painting for five grand."

"Ohmmmmghhn," I spluttered, feeling myself turn red with embarrassment.

"You'd better call them when you're feeling better," he said. "We must be paying you too much."

4. BANNER WAVING

*I*t was 7pm and I was standing at Heathrow Airport waiting for Ted to appear. He was due at any minute. The board said that his flight had landed, and that the bags were available to be collected.

"Why's it taking him so long to get his bag?" I spluttered at Veronica. I still had the paper towel in my cheek because I was terrified someone from work would see me without it and realise what a fraud I was.

"Please take that out," said Veronica. "No one from work is going to see you. You get too paranoid about things."

"It's not paranoia – I want to keep my job."

"Take it out," she insisted. "No one's going to take your damn job away."

She could be harsh sometimes, could Veronica. Being an ex-model she openly accepted that there was a catwalk bitch deep down inside her that emerged sometimes. Luckily, she was bloody lovely the rest of the time.

I dropped the sodden mess of tissue into my hand as surreptitiously as I could and put it into my pocket. They don't have bins in airports, so I was stuck with the damn thing.

"Well done," said Veronica, with a smile. "You look a lot better without it."

She had kindly come with me to meet Ted because I can't drive and she offered to be chauffeur for the evening. We both stood there in the glare of the harsh airport lighting, feeling as wrecked as each other.

Every so often she'd shake her head and say, "What are you going to do?" And I'd remember the nightmare hanging over me: art-gate. Veronica hadn't had a call, it was only me who had managed to win the auction. Bloody wonderful. I could no more afford to spend £5k on a piece of art than she could. Let's be honest, we couldn't afford to buy a bloody newspaper in the morning some days, never mind purchase glorious sketches from the world's greatest painters.

"We'll worry about that later," I said. "For now, I want to concentrate on Ted's homecoming. Do you think the sign's too much?"

Veronica shrugged. I knew she didn't think that holding up a sign was a good idea. She had already made that very clear.

The thing is, though, that I really wanted Ted to know how much I had missed him while he'd been away. If I rushed up to him waving a banner which said 'Welcome home, lovely Ted. I've missed you'...well, then he'd definitely know.

"Here he is," Veronica said. She sounded almost as excited as I was. Ted walked through looking remarkably po-faced and serious for such a tremendously fun-loving guy.

"Take this," I said to Veronica, throwing my handbag at her and rushing up to Ted, trailing the banner in the air behind me and chanting the letters of his name while dancing towards him. I felt a thrill of love and desire run through me. How could any woman resist this gorgeous bundle of masculinity?

Ted trundled along, all care-worn and tired. Despite being several stone overweight and dressed in an ill-fitting suit, to me he looked like a superhero. My lovely, handsome, perfect Super Ted.

"Give us a 'T', give us an 'e', give us a 'd'," I shouted, shaking my wrists to flutter the banner, and smiling like a fool.

As I got close, I saw the look of horror on Ted's face. He glanced to his side at the man standing next to him. I recognised him from the conference notes that Ted had shown me. Oh God, this was the important businessman whom Ted had been to Amsterdam to visit. What to do? I stood there, waving my sign while Ted looked mortified.

I don't know why I didn't just say hello and give him a hug, but I felt really embarrassed. More worryingly, I felt I was embarrassing Ted. I didn't want that. So instead of greeting him warmly as any other woman in the world would, I went skipping off, continuing to shout random letters until I'd gone right round the arrivals hall and was almost back where I started.

"Can I help you, ma'am?" said a security guard, standing alongside me.

"She's with me," said Ted, bravely. His important businessman friend couldn't have looked any more alarmed.

"Mary, meet Iars Peters," he said. "Iars, this is my lovely girlfriend Mary who I've been telling you all about."

"Very happy to meet," said Iars in a strong accent. "Ted is talking much about you."

"What's the matter with your face?" asked Ted, as Iars and I climbed into the back of Veronica's car. "Yes. Your cheek it is blue," said Iars.

"Yes, that's just makeup," I replied. "It's all very complicated."

Iars smiled and nodded, then stared at my face for the entire journey.

He was staying at the Hilton Hotel at Heathrow so we headed there first.

As we drove along, Veronica's phone rang and I saw the panic register on her face. She was a real stickler for driving sensibly and would never take a call while behind the wheel, so she passed the phone to Ted. "Would you answer that for me? It'll just be Mum – tell her I'll call her later." While my boyfriend took the phone, Veronica turned in to the hotel's driveway.

"Right," Ted was saying. "OK…"

Then he turned around and looked at Veronica quizzically. "It's some guy who says he needs to talk to you about the Picasso print you bought yesterday. He's been trying to reach you all day."

"Oh fuck," said Veronica, looking at me in the mirror.

THAT WAS 10 GRAND WE NEEDED TO FIND BETWEEN US.

5. LUNCH PLANS

"*Mary*, you are bonkers," summarised Ted when I told him about the fake operation, the blue makeup and the wad of cotton wool.

He pinched my nose affectionately and ruffled my hair, and suddenly everything felt OK. I loved having a boyfriend. Especially Ted because he was absolutely perfect. He was also fatter than me which was a bloody miracle. Imagine that – his thighs were wider than mine. That had never happened before.

"Come on," he said. "Tell me what happened."

"Well, it started when I went with Veronica to buy a dress so I could look nice for you when you came back."

"This is part of your LFBTTTCB campaign?"

"Yes." How embarrassing. I'd meant to take that note off the wall before he got back. "Anyway, I ripped the dress when I tried it on and I tried to buy it, but they wouldn't sell it to me. It was all very embarrassing."

Ted pulled me in closer to him and stroked my hair. I told him about the art exhibition and drinking too much and the fake operation and how I'd had to keep a wad of paper in my cheek all day. I explained that my cheek still really hurt so I had called in sick to save me having to do the paper in the cheek thing again.

"OK," he said.

"Am I really bad?"

"You are not at all bad," he said kindly. "A little bit bonkers sometimes, but definitely not bad. Perhaps I should join you today?"

"Ooooo," I replied, looking up at him wide-eyed.

"I was supposed to be going to lunch with Iars and five others from the office, but it's just a social thing. The deal won't be done today."

"That would be wonderful," I squealed.

"One moment," he said, and I heard him coughing and spluttering in the hallway as he explained his sudden onset flu to his bosses.

"All sorted," he said, coming back to bed and pulling me close to him. "So what on earth are we going to do to kill the time?"

The morning flew past in a whirl of passion, cuddles and chatting. We could happily have stayed in bed all day, but hunger eventually drove us from the sheets, and I headed into the kitchen.

"I don't know what food I've got in the cupboard," I said. "I was trying to diet, so didn't really buy anything."

"We could go out to lunch?" suggested Ted.

"Oh yes, yes, yes." I was thrilled with his idea. I've always loved eating out. I've always loved eating, to be fair, but it's always much more pleasurable when someone else is doing the work of cooking it. I bombarded Ted with suggestions, running through all the different restaurants we could go to. "There's this lovely pub where they do enormous jacket potatoes stuffed with cheese and bacon, or why don't we go to that place with the salad bar with all the lovely coleslaws and dressings on it, and those potato wedges they do as well and the delicious steaks."

"I've got a better idea," said Ted. "Why don't we go somewhere different, somewhere we've never been before, and see whether we can discover somewhere new and fantastic."

"OK," I said. "That sounds like a good idea, but please let's not go anywhere near the garden centre. I really don't want to bump into anyone there."

"We won't go anywhere near Cobham," said Ted. "Why don't we go to Putney or Barnes or somewhere like that? Let's go into London and see whether we can find somewhere wonderful to have lunch."

"Perfect," I replied.

"We don't have to go quite yet though, do we?" he said. I could feel his hands moving down my body.

"You are insatiable," I said, but inside I was delighted with the attention, the passion and adoration of this lovely man.

After 10 minutes of googling (no – that's not a euphemism) we discovered this gorgeous little place on the river in Fulham that sounded perfect. I printed off the directions, and we went in Ted's car, with me navigating. I was absolutely starving. If we didn't get there soon I'd start eating my hand.

"Left here," I shouted, sure that we could miss out loads of traffic if we went down a side road and cut out the main road.

"Good idea," said Ted, swinging the car left. "Oh look, that's Fulham Football Club."

Ted seemed to be waiting for me to comment. I didn't know what to say. I know absolutely nothing at all about football.

"We were just talking about Fulham the other day, weren't we?"

"I don't think so," I replied. "To be honest I don't think I've ever had a conversation about football with anyone in the whole world ever."

"Who on earth was I talking to about Fulham Football Club then?" he said to himself. "I can't for the life of me remember. I know someone was talking about the club."

"Can't help you, I'm afraid," I said, continuing to direct him to the pub on the river. I should point out at this stage that I have absolutely no sense of direction, I can't drive, I'm useless with maps, and I've never accurately directed anyone anywhere ever before. This was a triumph of unprecedented proportions. Ted pulled into the car parking space, put on the handbrake and smiled at me.

"We're here," he said. "You did well."

Did well? I was expecting a round of applause.

"That's the first time I've ever directed anyone and got them to the right place," I said. "Surely you have a brass band waiting to burst into a chorus of 'Congratulations'!"

"I might reward you with wine and food instead, if that's OK."

We walked into the pub garden and sat down at the table on a wooden decking area near the river. It was so beautiful. I do love London. I live on the edge of it, and should come into town more often, but it always feels like such an effort.

"I'm having the steak sandwich," said Ted after mulling over all the items on offer. I've no idea why the man looks at the menu. I've only been for a handful of meals with him but I can safely say that he always has the same thing. In Amsterdam he spent half an hour asking questions about the dishes. "Does the chicken come with pasta? What sort of sauce is this? Would it be possible to have the braised beef with rice instead of potatoes?" Then, after he'd asked a host of questions about all the food available, he had the steak.

"I'm going for the chicken and bacon salad," I said, nobly. I wanted the fish and chips like I've never wanted anything in my life before, but I reined myself in. I could easily nick some of Ted's chips.

He headed inside to place our orders while I sat back in my seat and looked out over the river with the sun on my face. This was the most relaxed I'd been for ages. A boat chugged slowly up the river. If only life could always be like this. The gentle sounds of the water and the light, sociable chatter of people in the garden. It was lovely.

"Hide, hide..."

My silent observations were ruined by shouts from the doorway, and the sight of a large man running out of the pub towards me. I turned round to see Ted – his face a picture of tortured concentration as he tore out of the pub like Usain Bolt. He plonked the drinks down, threw himself under the table and shouted for me to get under too.

"What on earth is the matter?" I asked.

"I'll tell you in a minute. Just make sure you can't be seen."

"OK," I said, slithering underneath. "Did you order our food?"

"Yes, but then I saw Iars."

"Iars? Shit. What is he doing here?"

"He's with the guys from work, including my boss, who I lied to this morning, pretending I had flu. This is a nightmare," said Ted. "He mustn't see me. Why the hell would they bring him to this place, of all the pubs in all of London?"

"Well it is very pretty on the river, perhaps they wanted to show him a nice part of London?"

"No, damn!" Ted shook his head as we both sat crouched under the table, bent over so we wouldn't bash our heads on the wood above us. "I remember now. He's a Fulham Football Club supporter. He was the one I was talking to about the club. Damn. They must've brought him to see the ground, then taken him to lunch."

"What are we going to do?" I asked. I was full of sympathy for Ted and his plight, and I could see that he needed not to be seen by his work colleagues in the pub, but I was also bloody uncomfortable and starving. If I didn't get my chicken and bacon soon I might shrivel up and die.

"I don't know, let's stay here a bit longer, and then work out what to do."

I reached up onto the table for my glass of wine and pulled it down so I could drink it while squatting underneath the table. It would have been so much nicer to sit in the chair with the sun on my face and the view of the river, but one glance at Ted's pained face reminded me not to comment, so I sat down on the wooden decking and tried to make myself comfortable.

As we sat, chatting quietly and dearly hoping not to be seen, a gang of people came along thinking the table was empty. They pulled out the chairs and went to sit down. Ted closed his eyes and shook his head. It was all too much for him.

"Um, hello, this is our table," I said, causing a woman clutching a bottle of wine to scream and leap back.

"What are you doing there?" she asked.

I had no idea how to answer her.

"Nothing," I said. "Could you please go to a different table."

"This is ridiculous," he mouthed at me. "This is the stupidest thing ever to happen to me in my whole, entire life."

I just shrugged. It wasn't the weirdest thing to have happened to me this week, so I wasn't in a position to comment.

"One steak sandwich with fries and one chicken and bacon salad," said the waitress. She could see us under the table, but was clearly unsure where we'd want our food to be placed.

"Under here, please," said Ted, as if it was the most natural thing in the world to be sitting underneath the table in a pub on the river in Fulham.

The waitress bent down and handed us our plates and cutlery. "Shall I put the condiments here?" She pointed to the floor and we both nodded. "Is there anything else?" she asked.

I could see she was very relieved when we both said no. I was also aware that she would go straight back inside and tell the other waiters and bar staff that there were mad people in the garden, sitting under the table. Meanwhile, Ted and I sat and ate our food, like toddlers who'd had a tantrum and were refusing to sit with their parents.

"We'll see the funny side to all this soon," I said to Ted, as he tore the steak sandwich apart.

"I'm never, ever, ever pretending to be ill ever again," he replied. "I'll have to really pull out all the stops at the weekend and make this deal happen, then if they have seen me under the table they won't care, they'll just focus on the fact that I've made them a fortune."

"At the weekend?" I tried not to sound alarmed. "You have to work at the weekend?"

"Didn't I say?" he replied. "I have to go back to Amsterdam at the weekend, to try and seal this deal."

6. YOUNG MAN, YOUR TESTICLES ARE IN MY FACE

I'd be lying if I said I wasn't disappointed that Ted would be away at the weekend. I'd been planning to talk to him about whether he'd come to meet my parents. Mum was desperate to see him. But I didn't want to come over as being a miserable girlfriend who was always moaning about things. And after the day we'd had – at that pub at lunchtime, sitting under the table – I thought it best to keep quiet and not moan.

"Fancy a glass of wine?" Ted asked. "Or are you still feeling rough from yesterday."

"I'm still feeling rough from yesterday, but yes, I would really love a glass of wine," I said, as Ted ruffled my hair and walked out towards the kitchen. He took a bottle of wine from the fridge and opened it, pouring generous helpings into two large glasses.

"As a special treat, can we sit on chairs tonight and not under the table?" I asked him.

"Ha ha," he said, handing me a glass of wine. "That was nuts, wasn't it? We should have just left."

"Na, it was more fun the way we did it," I reassured him.

He kissed me on the cheek and looked deep into my eyes. "Have I told you how beautiful you are?"

"And have I told you how handsome you are?" I replied as we clinked glasses. I took a large sip and that was when I had the best idea I'd ever had in my life. Why didn't I go out to Amsterdam, and meet Ted there? I could surprise him by turning up at his hotel. As I drank more, I refined the plan in my mind. Perhaps Veronica and I could go over, and have a girly night on Friday night and Saturday, then I could find Ted and surprise him, and we could all come back together on the Sunday. It felt like the best idea anyone had ever had.

"Where are you staying in Amsterdam?" I asked.

"Hotel Sebastian," he said. "Why?"

"No reason."

"And what are your plans while you're there?"

"Meetings during the day, dinner in the evening, then drinks in the hotel bar," he said. "Nothing too wild. Why?"

"No reason."

What could possibly go wrong?

Next morning my imaginary toothache having subsided completely, and the non-existent swelling having gone down, I was back at work. Ted's imaginary flu symptoms had disappeared as well, so he was in his office and preparing for his weekend trip to see Iars in Amsterdam. Little did he know that I was making similar plans to go to the capital of Holland.

Indeed, my day passed in a whirl of explaining to people that my injured mouth was now much better, and working out how I could get Veronica and me to Amsterdam for the least expense possible.

"By boat?" I texted to Veronica.

"Sure," she texted back. "Just as long as it's cheap."

The most economical way to travel was to get an overnight boat on Friday, followed by a train to Amsterdam on Saturday morning. It was so much cheaper than any other possible route. All we had to do was get down to the port on Friday night after work.

"I'll drive," said Veronica, and suddenly the whole thing was taking shape. The trip was cheap because we didn't need accommodation on the Friday night since we were on the boat. I just needed to find a cheap hotel room on the Saturday night and we'd be OK. But that was where I was coming unstuck. I kept rushing into the Ladies with my phone, to google hotels in Amsterdam but they were all so damn expensive.

Then Veronica stepped into the breach once more. "I have a tent," she said.

A tent? Perfect.

I booked us into a campsite and I felt a thrill of excitement run through me. We were going to bloody Amsterdam.

At 6.10pm on a busy Friday night, two very portly ladies stuffed themselves into a small Vauxhall Micra and headed for Harwich. The tent and many bags were safely stowed in the boot, along with sleeping bags and pillows. We had the tickets, passports and some hastily changed Euros, and we were off for a fun-filled weekend. We'd checked the luggage about a hundred times…the tent was there, the bags were there, and we had passport and tickets. This was going to be brilliant.

Pink came on to the radio and Veronica whacked up the volume. We were rock stars, singing along; laughing, cheering and clapping. This was going to be the best weekend of our lives. Guaranteed. And the great thing about it was that Ted had absolutely no idea we were coming. He'd have the surprise of his life and be so delighted when he saw me there. It was going to be enormous.

In the interests of subterfuge, I had resisted the urge to post anything about our trip on Facebook, in case he saw it. I'm normally the sort of person who charts her entire life through Facebook. This time I just posted:

"Quiet weekend ahead, looking forward to relaxing and doing nothing."

I got a couple of offensive comments on the post, with friends writing: "Possibly the most boring update ever on Facebook?" and "Could you be any duller, Mary?"

But they don't know… They have no idea what we are going to get up to in the land of clogs, bicycles and Edam cheese.

Veronica pulled into the car park and we clambered out and retrieved all our gear from the boot, checking it one more time: tent – check, bags – check, sleeping bags – check. We had everything. We could barely carry it all, but we had it.

Having thought that I should go for comfort rather than glamour on the boat, I now felt quite ridiculously dressed. We didn't have a cabin so were sleeping on reclining seats, and I thought that getting to sleep would be much easier if I wore something soft and snugly. My baby pink velour onesie had seemed like the only option for guaranteed comfort, and with boots and shades, I thought I'd be able to get away with it, but now I felt stupid. Especially since Veronica was so much more soberly dressed in a white shirt and jeans. Her great poise, elegance and height could all be a bit distressing at the best of times, but more so when I'm head to foot in powder pink. Every time I caught sight of us in the shop windows I looked as if I was her overgrown toddler. I really wished I had worn something less obvious.

Hopefully my decision to opt for comfort over any semblance of style would yield rewards when it was bedtime and Veronica was struggling to get comfortable in tight jeans while I was sleeping like a baby.

We boarded the boat simply and easily, and found a good spot where we would base ourselves. Near to the bar, but not so close as to be noisy and crowded-out, near the action, but not in the centre of it.

"This has all come together much more easily than I thought it would," I said to Veronica.

"I know," she said. "To be honest, I thought it would be a miracle if we made it to the boat…let alone with all our luggage and on time!"

"We should celebrate," I declared, and Veronica gave me the thumbs up.

"Wine?"

"Yes please, my lovely," she said. "But let's try not to drink too much."

"Agreed."

We had spoken earlier in the week about how we would try our hardest not to get horribly drunk overnight on the boat. We had a big day ahead in Amsterdam, then a Saturday night with Ted. We didn't want to ruin the whole weekend because we had hangovers.

"Let's have a rule," I suggested. "For every alcoholic drink, we must have a soft one, so we alternate, and don't just drink booze all night."

"Good idea," said Veronica. "That's a really good idea. Yes." So I went up to the bar to buy us our wines, knowing that the next round would consist of soft drinks to keep us on the straight and narrow.

We finished our first glasses, cheering as the boat left and we were on our way to the Hook of Holland. I'd soon be in the same country as Ted. It was all fiercely exciting.

Veronica went up to the bar and came back with our second drinks of the trip. You'll remember that these were supposed to be non-alcoholic but I fear that my lovely friend didn't quite understand the plan. She came back with a whole tray of drinks: soft drinks and alcoholic drinks.

"We down the soft drinks as quickly as possible, so we can get on to the wine." She plonked the tray onto the table.

"Great," I said, and this was how we proceeded through the evening, with me going to the bar next, buying two large glasses of wine and a small lemonade. We split the lemonade between two glasses and knocked it back, then carried on with the wine drinking. My great plan to cut the number of alcoholic drinks in half was failing miserably; we were just consuming sugary soft drinks as well. But we were having such a great time that it was difficult to feel too upset about it.

"What's Ted going to say when he sees us?" asked Veronica. "Will he be really shocked?"

"Definitely," I replied. Ted would be utterly thrown by our appearance. I knew him well enough to know that he'd be really pleased though. He'd be shocked and speechless, but really happy.

Veronica and I had relaxed into our new environment and were confident we could sleep in the reclining chairs, especially given how much wine we were drinking. The only thing we weren't so keen on was how young everyone on the boat was. Most of them were in their teens or early 20s, all packed around the bar knocking back shots and chasers and generally getting hammered far more quickly and more noisily than we were.

"I feel like a bloody pensioner," said Veronica, and I knew what she meant. It was a very odd experience. If there's one thing that can be guaranteed in this world it is that when I'm drinking, I'm usually drinking more than anybody else. Look at the size of me, for goodness' sake. You don't get to my size drinking water and nibbling ice cubes.

Veronica came back from the bar with our latest trayful and plonked it down.

"This is a party boat," she said.

"What do you mean, a party boat?"

"That's what it is. It's a booze cruise and most of the people are on it are either celebrating their 18th birthday parties or 21st birthdays. No wonder we feel like two little old ladies."

"What happens on party boats?" I asked, fearing the night of debauchery ahead of us.

"According to the barman, there will be wrestling in jelly and naked bar walking later. The barman just asked me whether you were planning to enter the wet t-shirt competition later."

"Good God, is he insane?"

"I told him you wouldn't want to and he looked really disappointed."

By 3am there was no doubt that we were on a party boat. Veronica and I had tried to be good sports, we really had, but we were far too old to want to dance the night away or get fondled by amorous teenagers. I had managed to win a bottle of unbelievably disgusting 'champagne' from having a bloke's testicles dangled into my face. Before you judge me – I wasn't aware that I had agreed to this, I wasn't even aware that it was going to happen. The barman announced something, everyone started chanting and looking over at us, so I waved. Veronica smiled and waved too. We were just being friendly. Next thing, everyone was slow clapping and he shouted,

"Will you?" I looked at him hopelessly and he repeated, "Come on, lady in pink – say you will."

I said "OK" fearing that I'd have to dance with an 18-year-old, but instead there was a loud cheer and a young man clambered onto the table next to our reclined seats. He pulled down his trousers, straddled my face and I had his horrible, wrinkly, teenage balls in my face before I could think straight. Then I was stuck. What could I do? Sitting up would have brought me into even closer proximity, so I closed my eyes, ignored them, and waited for him to get off. When he finally dismounted, I turned to Veronica; her eyes were out on stalks.

"What the fuck are you doing?" she asked.

"We must never speak of this again," I said. "Never."

"OK. But...what? Why did you do that? Who are you?"

"I got stuck," I said. "I was embarrassed and confused. I didn't know what to do."

The guy who'd dangled his bits in my face handed me my bottle of 'champagne', then turned to his friend. "That's the first time I've had my bollocks in a really fat girl's face," he said, and they both laughed heartily as they walked back towards the bar.

I felt like shit. I rolled over on the seat, curled up and pretend to go to sleep. I was drunk, tired and felt horrible. It was all my own fault so I wasn't looking for any sympathy, but as I closed my eyes against the wild partying on the boat, I thought about how horrible it was to be 'the fat girl' that they were all laughing at, and I started to cry.

I'd been 'the fat girl' for years. And I knew why... it was because whenever anything went even remotely wrong, I'd find myself eating huge amounts of food before I'd even realised what was happening. My mum would say something about my hair looking funny or someone at work would tell me I hadn't put the plants in the right place, and I'd feel devastated and the need to stuff myself with food until I just couldn't feel anything more would completely overwhelm me. Until I'd forced the feelings down with food, I couldn't cope. I'd feel like I'd got something missing – the resilient bit that allowed me to ignore little barbs or slights... And I suspected I knew where that came from…from an incident in a gymnastics club many years ago when I was an innocent little girl.

I wiped my eyes with the backs of my hand and tried to fall asleep before Veronica could see that I was upset. We'd soon be in Holland. Everything would be OK. I'd lose the weight. I'd lose it and no one would ever laugh at me for being fat again.

Morning came along with all the subtlety and elegance of a nuclear missile landing on my face. The sun streamed in through the windows, lighting up the interior of the boat which, frankly, couldn't have looked in a worse state if it had crashed in the night. If you moved anything it would be tidier. There were bottles, cans, clothes and bodies lying across the seats, on the floor and on the bar. Two hardy young men still stood at the bar drinking, while all around them people had collapsed.

Two cleaners had attempted to enter the fray and were trying to impose a modicum of order over the place, but the bodies lying all over the floor prevented them from doing anything but pick up litter and collect glasses to return to the bar area. The loudspeaker announced our arrival in Holland, as Veronica and I squinted into our compact mirrors and reapplied makeup that we had never taken off the night before.

"Well, I've looked better." Veronica licked her finger and wiped it across her eyelid. "This is not a luxurious way to travel."

"No," I agreed quickly. "This booze cruise might be the worst decision we have ever made in our lives."

We joined the line of people exiting the boat, all of them looking as ropey as us. Men unshaven, women with smeared mascara across their faces, all of them piggy eyed and regretting last night's excesses.

"Right," said Veronica, putting the bags down to give her arms a break. "We can do this, all we have to do is get on the train to Amsterdam. That can't be too hard, can it?"

"It can't be," I agreed. "Once we're in Amsterdam, we can get our tent set up and relax. The hardest bit's over now."

We walked towards the train station and saw a big sign saying 'Trains to Amsterdam'.

"Brilliant," I said. Even we couldn't mess this up. All we had to do was get on the first train that came.

But Veronica had stopped and was looking open-mouthed at her bags.

"What's the matter?" I asked.

"It's the tent," she replied. "I've left it on the boat."

"Oh God no. We have to have the tent. We can't afford any of those hotels. Run back and get it and I'll wait here with the bags."

"Don't go anywhere." She turned and legged it back to the boat, weaving her way through the teenagers disembarking around her.

I had no idea whether they would allow her back on, or whether the tent would be there when she got to our seats. It might have been cleared away by the cleaners or nicked by drunk teenagers. I crossed my fingers that she would find it. We were buggered without it.

I heard Veronica running back onto the platform before I saw her. She had the tent in her arms and a look of sheer victory on her face. "Got it," she announced, holding it up like the FA Cup. "Let's go to Amsterdam."

The next train was only 10 minutes away, so we sat on the platform and talked about how much we never wanted to go on a party boat ever again.

"I've never felt so old and unadventurous before," I said.

"You were *quite* adventurous." Veronica raised her eyebrows at me.

"We said we would never speak of it," I chided.

"We won't," said Veronica. "Never."

7

MORE CAKE, PLEASE

*G*osh, Amsterdam was beautiful. I wasn't expecting it to be quite so stunning. I'd heard all the stories about the sex museum and prostitutes around every corner, and feared I might get drafted into some whorehouse. As it turned out it was all gorgeous waterside cafes, people cycling around without fear for their life from London traffic, and an air of sophisticated, but friendly nonchalance. There was this general aura of happiness and joviality that permeated. It was really nice. It would have been much better if Veronica and I hadn't felt like a couple of old guys who'd just been through the D-Day landings. Honestly, I'd never felt so rough in my life.

"I need coffee," I said. "I can't do anything before I've had some caffeine."

"Me too," Veronica agreed, so we stumbled, with our many bags in hand, into the nearest cafe.

"You have got the tent, haven't you?" I said to her for the five hundredth time that day. I was so paranoid after she'd left it on the boat.

"Yes," she said, holding it up for me to see. "I won't lose it again. I know we're buggered without it."

"Two coffees, please," said Veronica in her best Dutch (obviously – no Dutch at all).

"Anything to eat?" said the waiter, his accident beautifully Dutch, but his words English.

"Oh yes please. I'm starving," said Veronica, looking at me nervously. "I have to eat something."

"Yes, me too," I said, surreptitiously. The subject of eating is always a difficult one. We'd met at Fat Club, for God's sake. We weren't able to negotiate eating very easily.

"What have you got that we could have for breakfast? What's typically Dutch?" I asked. "I mean – what are you famous for here?"

"Maybe this cake?" he said. "We are very famous for this space cake."

"Special cake? Which special cake?"

He walked over to the cabinet and pointed to a nice-looking cake.

"Is it good?"

"Very good indeed," he said.

"We will have two, and two cappuccinos," I said. I felt so guilty that I couldn't look at Veronica.

"Don't worry," she reassured me. "We'll get back on that diet soon."

The waiter came to our table with a tray laden with our coffees and cakes. "Enjoy," he said.

Veronica peeled a piece of the cake off and put it into her mouth. "Yum, I'm bloody starving."

I took a large sip of coffee and watched as Veronica nibbled at the cake. I needed caffeine first, and I felt so guilty and annoyed with myself at ordering cake that now I felt bad eating it.

"I'm just going to the loo," I said, heading through the side door and out to the bathroom where I was entertained by a large map of Amsterdam on the door, with the key places to go circled with what looked like a bright red lipstick. I looked at them, they were all places we'd thought of going. Perhaps we should hire bicycles? Once we'd dropped our stuff off at the campsite we'd be free to cycle around all day. I rather liked the idea of that. It would be worth me checking with Veronica.

But when I walked back into the cafe, Veronica took one look at me and burst into laughter. "Where the hell have you been?" she yelled out.

"I've just been to the loo," I replied, far more quietly than she was being.

She laughed so much she nearly fell off her chair, banging the table with her hand, as she creased over. "The loo?" she said. "I can't believe you've gone to the loooooo."

What the hell was going on?

Veronica turned to the waiter who was serving the only other two people in the cafe. Thank God it was empty. Veronica screamed at the top of her voice: "My friend has been to the loo," before dissolving into peals of laughter again.

I sat down nervously and began to sip my coffee.

"Why are you screaming and shouting?" I asked.

"Why is your head not on properly?" she responded. "Your head is all wonky and it looks like it's going to fall off."

Before I could answer, she ran round the table and held my head between her hands. "I'm here just in time, I got here just-in-time," she said. "Your head nearly fell off. You haven't thanked me for saving it."

She rushed back to her chair, and sat back into it, nearly falling off backwards.

I nibbled at the cake, and drank my coffee while Veronica examined her thumbs, laughing occasionally about how they weren't hers at all. She wrote 'I love you' in the air with her finger and I ate my cake as quickly as possible so we could get out of there and get Veronica into the fresh air.

But no. NO. Veronica was right. It was very funny. My thumbs were on backwards too. Wooow...how did that happen?

It was so funny. I roared with laughter as I watched Veronica writing in the sky with someone else's fingers.

"Are your thumbs from a magic bird?" I asked her.

But there was no time to wait for the answer; her head was wobbling... I rushed over. Perhaps if I brushed her hair, her head would stay on her shoulders. But when I got to her head, the sight of all the hairs coming out of it was the funniest thing I'd ever seen. "Why have you got so much hair?" I said, laughing so much my stomach was hurting as I fell to my knees behind her, clutching a hairbrush. "You've got so much hair it's ridiculous. I'm going to count them one by one and see how many there are. I'll start at the top."

I tried to stand up in order to begin my counting but the floor was moving and I kept slipping and Veronica was laughing so much. Was she laughing because she had so much hair? Probably. The waiter came along and helped me to my feet, taking me to my chair and sitting me down. I looked at him and suddenly realised that he was the guy who played Superman in the film. Wow! What was he doing here?

"I need your autograph. You are Superman," I said. "How did you get to be Superman? Wow, I can't believe it, you're serving coffee and you're Superman."

"Just you have a sit down I'll bring you some water," he said.

"Go, Superman, get me some water."

At the next table the man and woman were looking over at us.

"She has loads of hair all over her head and he is Superman!" I screamed across the cafe. They seemed uninterested. They just smiled at me and went back to their drinks. How could people not be interested in the fact that Superman was serving coffee?

"There you go, ladies," said the waiter, as he brought us large glasses of water. He was definitely Superman. "Next time maybe just have one hash cake between you?"

How we left the cafe is a mystery to me. I remember going to cross the road, and thinking it was really funny when the little green man appeared. Veronica and I clutched each other in the street – howling, laughing and pointing at the little green man.

Then we seemed to have found a bench and we were sitting there, laughing. And we couldn't really move from the bench, so we closed our eyes and drifted slowly off to sleep.

We woke a couple of hours later, disorientated and confused.

"What the hell?" I asked. "I mean…what happened then?"

"Hash cake," said Veronica. "It's cake with cannabis in it. They call it space cake."

"It was the weirdest experience of my life," I said. Not particularly unpleasant, just weird. "And you do have a lot of hairs on your head."

It was at that point that we realised we'd lost the tent.

It fell to Veronica to return to the cafe and find the tent, since she was the one charged with looking after it. She stood up from the bench, stumbled a little, then weaved her way across the crowded street and back to the cafe.

She came back minutes later, grinning. She held the tent in one hand and a bag in the other.

"I couldn't resist it," she said, waving her grocery bag in front of me. In it she had two more hash cakes. "Let's have these when we've got the tent all set up."

8

CAMPING CATASTROPHE

*A*msterdam was staggeringly beautiful. Have I mentioned that yet? It really was. I'd read the literature before we went, of course, and I knew that it had more canals than Venice, but what the tourist brochure couldn't explain was just what an incredible impact those canals had on the look and feel of the place. They seemed to weave through the city like a living, breathing animal. Then there was the beauty of the bridges, changing the landscape as you looked across the city. And did I mention all the gabled houses? They were lovely.

I felt I could live in the city. In fact, I thought I might never go home, and perhaps Ted and I could move out to Amsterdam?

I pictured myself cycling around all day and losing loads of weight, then rowing down the river with Ted in the evening and meeting up with friends for supper in one of the fabulous cafes. There was such a lovely feel to the city, perhaps because it was quite small, so nowhere was too far away, and you kept seeing people you'd just met. It meant that within hours of being there, we felt like we knew people, and understood the place.

The best part of it all was the cafe culture. Cafe after cafe next to each other, with people just chilling, reading their books, and minding their own business. In England people would sit at home, watching daytime TV and feeling lonely. Here, people came out and listened to their music, read their books or chatted with passers-by. It all felt so much more healthy than the way we lived in England. Because everyone seemed to be out, there was so much to see, with people cycling past and tourists walking over the bridges, stopping to stare at the beauty of it all.

Our campsite was on the edge of town, a short bus ride from all the attractions of the city centre, and just a couple of miles, by my reckoning, from the hotel in which Ted was staying. In other words, it was perfect. It also looked clean and was buzzing as lots of people arrived and set themselves up. We went to the reception area and collected the token which allowed us to proceed.

"Here we go," suggested Veronica, pointing towards a lovely wide space in which we could set up the tent and have plenty of room to sit out on deckchairs, chat and put the world to rights. It was quite near to the toilet block where we would want to go and change into our finery later, but not so close that we would be greeted by the stench of urine at all times.

"Perfect," I said, noticing no children nearby, no groups of rowdy men, and a little pathway both to the toilet block and to the exit. "I think you might have just found the most perfect place in the world." We high-fived in our excitement.

I opened my bag which contained the sleeping bags rolled up tightly, and the small pillows that we could blow up. No luxuries had been spared. This was going to be magnificent.

"Let's get this tent set up, then we can go off and explore for a bit," said Veronica, pulling poles from the tent bag and the sheet of canvas. I looked at it all, and was filled with fear.

I remembered my own camping holidays as a child, with my parents on the brink of divorce by the time they got the tent up.

"No, Marina, that is not where it goes," my dad would howl.

"If you're so brilliant at this, Martin, why don't you just do it yourself and I'll take the children for a walk along the beach," Mum would yell back.

"I'm not saying I'm brilliant," Dad would reply. "It's just that if you hold it there we won't be able to stretch it over the poles..." And so the arguments would continue for what felt like hours. My parents would battle with the tent, and then with one another, until finally, finally the tent was up.

But that was my parents...and I had confidence in us: Veronica and I were reasonably intelligent women, and the tent was much smaller so would be far less hassle. I looked at bits of rope, canvas and loads of poles, and I couldn't for the life of me work out how we were going to turn this collection into a beautiful tent that would house us overnight.

"Do you want to take the poles and assemble them?" Veronica said.

I couldn't help but think I'd been dealt the short straw. Wasn't it all about the poles? Wasn't I basically now in charge of the whole tent?

"I'll sort out the pegs and the canvas," she said.

I had no idea what to do. I assumed there would be enough poles to create a base square and then I would build two arches over the top onto which the canvas would be stretched, and pinned down with the pegs. But basic maths indicated that there were nowhere near enough poles for this to happen. Perhaps there was just one arch over the top?

I looked at the poles again. I couldn't see how there was even a base square let alone an arch.

"I don't really know how to do this," I said. None of the poles seemed to have bends in them. How would I make them into anything? And there were so few of them. There seemed to be a lot of string. Perhaps the string linked between the poles or something?

I turned to Veronica who was looking as puzzled as I was feeling.

"There don't seem to be enough poles," I told her. "There is a lot of string, does the string link the poles together or something? If so, we are going to need instructions because I've no idea how to do it."

"I don't know," she said in dismay. "There doesn't seem to be anything like enough canvas. And the tent is blue. I thought it was red before. I don't understand."

We stared at the poles which would no more make a tent base than I would make a nuclear scientist, and the square of canvas that would no more provide a covering than Veronica would make the next President of the United States. A young family walked past, nodding, smiling and wishing us a good morning, as people on campsites are prone to do.

They sounded English, so I ran over towards them, asking for help.

"I'm so sorry to interrupt your walk, but we are completely baffled here. Have you ever seen a tent like this before?" I asked. "If you could just point me in the right direction as to how it comes together, I'd be really grateful. I can't make any sense out of it."

"Sure," said the man. "I'll take a look."

I could see the woman was a bit pissed off, but we wouldn't keep them long, I just needed a steer as to how this thing came together.

A loud guffaw from the man as he looked at our collection of poles and canvas indicated that things weren't going to run smoothly from here on in.

"Is there a problem?" I asked.

The man laughed again. "Well it depends whether you want to camp tonight."

"Yes, this is our tent," I replied.

"You won't be doing any camping in this. This is a kite," he said. "It's quite a nice kite, the kids would love to come over and play with it later, if you're taking it out on the beach, but you're not going to make a tent out of it."

"Oh God," said Veronica. "I must have picked up the wrong bag. My mum said it was in the loft, so I went up into the loft and got it."

"It did seem quite small." I remembered that I had commented on how compact it was, but Veronica had said that it was the latest in modern lightweight camping equipment.

"Do you like flying kites?" she asked.

"No," I replied. "I can't think of anything I'd less like to do right now than fly a kite on the beach."

"Hash cake?" said Veronica, palming off half a cake on to me.

I looked at her and smiled. "Yep, let's eat hash cake," I replied.

And so that's how we ended up in the sex museum.

9

STATIC TENTS

*W*e found there were only so many times that you could witness sex acts of extraordinary weirdness in the course of a gentle afternoon in Amsterdam. Even when we'd had half a hash cake each and found our own feet so funny that we were crying with laughter, it still wasn't *that* entertaining.

The bizarre views on display in the museum were just obtuse. Perhaps I'm a big prude, but I don't need to see animals of different breeds at it with one another and I certainly have no desire to watch humans frolicking with farmyard beasts.

Veronica and I fumbled our way through the ground floor of the museum, then decided the escalator to the upper floors was all too much for us. Things were spinning and I'd taken against the darkness. I needed fresh air or I was going to be sick, so we staggered back through the art section, the toys section and another section which didn't seem to have any unifying theme (or any redeeming features, to be honest) and left the museum. I'm not saying we didn't enjoy it – it was fun – it was just that once you'd seen one man on all fours, bound and gagged and wearing a fake penis, you'd seen them all. You certainly didn't need to see another 20.

"What now?" asked Veronica.

111

"We could try and see whether there's a really cheap B&B, or youth hostel or something?" I said.

She shrugged her shoulders and raised her eyebrows in a manner which indicated that was the very last thing she wanted to do with an evening in Amsterdam.

"A bed-and-breakfast sounds better than a bloody youth hostel."

I couldn't disagree. I pulled out my phone and started googling reasonably priced B&Bs in the centre of Amsterdam. The only ones which came anywhere near the descriptor 'reasonable' were ones that were buried deep in the heart of the red-light district.

"Can you rent tents?" I asked.

"Oh, that's not a bad idea," said Veronica. "In fact, that's a very good idea. I wonder whether you can?"

Back onto Google we went. Yes, generally speaking, you could hire tents but could you hire one with no notice in the middle of Amsterdam? It seemed not. Then, I saw it.

"There's a campsite with fixed tents in it," I said. "That would be good. We wouldn't have to put it up or anything."

"Is it glamping?" asked Veronica.

"I have no idea what that is," I replied.

"It's posh camping...glamorous camping...nice tents with fridges and televisions and heating and stuff."

"Oh. I don't know. It doesn't say. It just says that the campsite we were at earlier has tents there that are permanent, so you don't have to bring one with you."

"So, the choice is – go back to the campsite and set ourselves up there, or ring Ted and explain that we're here and don't have a tent."

I know that Veronica thought I should ring Ted, but I couldn't go and see him while still dressed in a pink onesie that I'd been wearing all night.

I was also aware that Ted was working out here. He was signing a huge deal and didn't want great big distractions from it.

"This is Ted's big break," I said to Veronica. "You know, he's worked his way up from post boy to become a really important salesman in the company, and he takes it all very seriously. When he came back from Amsterdam last time and took a day off to spend with me, he felt so madly guilty about it that he's been working 20-hour days ever since. He is in Amsterdam because a big Dutch company is interested in buying his software, and if they do it'll be a multi-million pound deal for Ted's company, and confirm him as a hugely successful salesman. It would also earn him a whacking great bundle of money on commission."

I didn't think me storming in there uninvited this afternoon dressed like Miss Piggy would help him at all.

I continued. "I haven't showered or washed my hair and I've consumed nothing but hash cakes and alcohol since midday yesterday. I don't want to see him like this."

"OK," said Veronica. "But shall we eat the other hash cake while we think about it?"

"No," I said, determinedly. "Let's go back to the campsite, get one of their fixed tents, stick our stuff in it, then eat the hash cake." I was becoming so sensible I was scaring myself.

The day was getting on. It was almost 1pm and I wanted to be looking bloody brilliant by tonight. We needed to get ourselves into the campsite and showered and changed or this whole weekend was going to collapse around our ears.

"And we should probably pick up something for lunch," I added.

"Yes," said Veronica. "Let's do that."

We nodded at one another proudly.

"We can be sensible if we try," she said.

"Yes," I agreed.

But then we ate the hash cake.

10

WE FINALLY GET TO SEE TED

*A*t least we were in the tent. Neither of us could remember how we got there. We remembered sitting on the bench, and I remembered standing up and looking at the map and declaring that we ought to leave and find the campsite. I remembered Veronica finding this funny, of course, but then Veronica was finding everything funny by this stage. What I couldn't remember was how on earth we got here. How did we know which bus to get or when to get off, or anything like that?

I vaguely remembered arriving at the campsite, and I remembered there being some confusion at reception because we couldn't stop laughing enough to tell the man that we had booked a static tent.

"You have a tent," he said, pointing to Veronica's bag.

"It's a kite," we said, roaring with laughter. Really, everything was funny.

Somehow we made him understand that we needed a static tent, and somehow we found the right one and were now in it.

Along the way we must have bought food because two paper bags lay next to us. I sat up and pulled one towards me, waking Veronica as the paper rustled.

"I'm so starving I'm going to die," she said.

"Don't die," I replied, handing her a bag.

"Oh wow, thanks, you've been out to get food. You superstar."

"No, we bought it earlier, I think," I said. "It was here when I woke up."

It was worrying that neither of us had any recollection of buying the food.

Inside the bags were sandwiches (carbs, calories), with butter on (fat, calories) and stuffed with ham and cheese (more fat, more calories and some protein), there were crisps and cans of Coke (of the non-diet variety).

Veronica and I froze as if we'd found live snakes in the bags. "Full-fat," I said.

"But we have to eat," she said. "We'll both be ill if we don't."

"OK," I said. "But this has to stay between us. We must never mention this in front of Fat Club people."

"I swear," said Veronica, solemnly. "I'll tell people about the hash cakes and the sex museum but I will never, ever talk about the full-fat Coke."

"Or what happened on the boat," I said.

"I've already forgotten about the bloke on the boat dangling his testicles in your face, so don't worry about that."

"Good," I replied.

The food was delicious. You know how utterly lovely it is to eat when you're really hungry, and oooo...we were hungry. I loved every last bit of our little picnic.

"I feel so much better now," said Veronica.

"Good, me too. Food's great, isn't it? I mean – it really is great."

Veronica nodded and pushed back her sleeve to look at her watch. "Christ. It's 4pm," she said. "How did it get to 4pm?"

"I don't know. We could do with making a plan of some sort."

I agreed. We needed to work out what the hell to do. Veronica pulled out a map of Amsterdam.

"Right, this is where Ted is," I explained, pointing out Hotel Sebastian on the map.

Veronica marked it with a red pen.

"Here we are," I said.

She marked our campsite with her red pen.

"I think it will take us about 45 minutes to get to his hotel," I concluded.

"When should we leave?"

"Ted is going out for an early supper with Iars, the guy we met at the airport, and will be back at the hotel by 8.30pm."

"He gets back at 8.30? Are you sure? That's a really early supper," she said.

"Iars is on the red-eye to New York later, so they have to meet early. Why don't we get to his hotel while he's out at his dinner and have a few drinks in the bar, then when he comes back we scream 'surprise' and he'll be so pleased to see us he'll almost wet himself."

"That seems to me to be a simple, logical, straightforward plan." Veronica's eyes were brimming with trust and respect.

I raised my eyebrow at her.

"No, seriously," she said. "It's the sort of plan that won't go wrong."

And in that moment, something deep within me screamed: 'THE PLAN IS GOING TO GO WRONG!'

FIRST JOB WAS TO GO TO THE TOILET BLOCK AND SHOWER AND DRESS. I'D been dying for a shower all day and was starting to feel pretty revolting in my grubby, stained pink onesie, so was delighted when we made our way there and found the block clean and empty. Hooray! No queuing for the showers. We each went into a cubicle and I laid out my shower gel, shampoo, conditioner and shaving foam. I retrieved my razor from the bottom of the toiletries bag and put that on the end of the line.

"Is your shower working?" asked Veronica.

"I don't know yet." It had taken me a couple of minutes to lay out my tools. I pressed the red button and nothing happened. I turned it. Still nothing. "There's no water coming out," I shouted.

"I know," said Veronica. "I'm just trying another one but that's not working either."

Bollocks.

I slipped on my pink onesie, gathered my ruck sack and other possessions and walked outside to meet Veronica. "What are we going to do?" I asked.

"Let's go to the reception and tell them," she said.

The reception area was busy with people chatting away in Dutch.

"Excuse me," said Veronica, spelling out her question, using mime and over-exaggerated language.

"Only seven and nine," said the man.

Veronica and I looked at one another. Neither of us had a clue what this meant.

"Showers," I tried, moving my hand above my head to mimic the falling water.

"Seven and nine, two times," said the man.

Finally a kindly English-speaking man explained. "The showers are only open between seven and nine in the morning, and seven and nine in the evening at this time of year."

"Seven?" Veronica shouted at him, as if the shower situation was wholly his fault.

"Yes," he replied. "It says it in all the literature. Most campsites are the same."

"Bugger," said Veronica. "Is there no water at all? I mean, even cold water?"

"No shower," said the man behind the counter, turning to the next person in the queue.

We walked off, back to our tent. Back to make a new plan.

We seemed to be going through plans like we were going through hash cakes...at reckless speed.

"OK," said Veronica. "We need to be showered and changed before we go out tonight."

"Yes," I agreed.

"But there are no showers here."

"Indeed not."

"So I suggest we go to Hotel Sebastian and shower there. What do you think?"

I wasn't convinced it was the greatest plan ever, but I was struggling to think of an alternative. "We'll have to get there early," I said.

"Yes, we'll get there for 6pm, then there'll be no way that we can bump into Ted because he'll already be out to supper."

"True," I said.

"We'll use the hotel showers (we'd googled this; there was a spa section in the hotel that we planned to sneak into). We'll get ready, then we'll sit in the bar, looking awesome, awaiting Ted's return."

AT 6PM WE WENT TO HOTEL SEBASTIAN AND WANDERED IN, TRYING TO look as natural as possible and as if we were guests while we looked for the spa area. The only problem was that we were still dressed in yesterday's yucky clothes and carrying backpacks. We didn't blend in at all with the smart Dutch women who drifted through the reception area.

"There," said Veronica, seeing a sign for the spa.

We walked over to it as nonchalantly as possible, but when Veronica tried the door it didn't open. She tried again. I tried. Nope. It wasn't opening. Suddenly it dawned on us...you needed your room key to access the spa.

There was no sign of any other showers anywhere.

"OK," said Veronica. "Don't panic. This is going to be OK. Let's just sit on this sofa and wait until someone comes to use the spa, then when they open the door, we'll pile in."

"A bit like we did with the art gallery?" I suggested.

"A bit like that."

"Because that ended up being so successful," I said.

But there was no alternative. So we sat there.

"I wish we had some hash cake," said Veronica.

"You have a problem," I said. "Forget Fat Club, you need to go to Hash Cake Club."

Then, finally, along came an elderly couple. The man flicked his room key against the lock and the door flew open. Veronica and I flew up, we dashed towards the spa and bundled in behind them, arriving just in time to get in before the door closed. Inside we were greeted by a woman in a white shirt and trousers, ticking off room numbers in the book.

"We're with them," said Veronica, pointing at the elderly couple.

"With whom?" asked the assistant.

We both looked up to point at the couple in front of us. They were disappearing into the changing area as two men walked out.

"Oh hell," Veronica said.

"Oh bloody, bloody hell," I said.

It was Ted and Iars.

I was dressed in a dirty pink onesie, hadn't washed all day and my hair was all over the place. I'd had a conversation with Ted earlier in which I'd told him I was in Tesco's in Esher. Now, here I was, about to get thrown out of a spa in Amsterdam.

Veronica and I instinctively stood still. Hoping he wouldn't notice us if we didn't flinch. Like if you see a bear in the woods, you keep still and he won't notice you're there.

Except Ted isn't a bear, and he could see me very clearly.

"Mary, what the hell are you doing here?" he asked. "Why have you followed me to Amsterdam? And what on earth are you wearing?"

"Oh God," I said to Veronica as quietly as I could. "I don't know what to say…"

"You need to say something," she whispered. "I'll back you up. Just say anything."

"It was all Veronica's idea." But judging by the look of alarm on Veronica's face, that wasn't what she was expecting when she said 'anything'. "Veronica had to come to Amsterdam for work, so I thought I'd come with her. Sorry to take you by surprise, I was planning to call you later and see whether you wanted to meet for a drink."

I looked at Veronica, appealing with my eyes for the help she'd promised me earlier. She looked like she'd just been punched. "Yes," she said, eventually. "All my fault."

"Oh no, no one's fault at all. It's lovely to see you both. You just took us by surprise, that's all. You should have called earlier. Are you staying in this hotel?"

"No, not quite," I replied. "We had a bit of a problem with our accommodation, to be honest. The hotel that Veronica's work booked us into burned down. Completely burned to the ground. Nothing left of it – just ashes."

It was alarming how easily I was able to conjure these lies. I've always thought myself a particularly bad liar, but it turns out that under pressure they come streaming out of me. It's a relief in many ways. It means that if there's ever another world war and the Germans capture me, there's every chance that I'll instinctively lie and not give away the whereabouts of the British army.

"Do you two want to come up and use my room to change?" asked Ted. "I'll go and talk to the receptionist and find out which room Mark was in. He never showed up because his mum was ill, so there's a room we've paid for and aren't using."

"That's brilliant," I said, looking at Veronica, who had happily shaken off the look of utter disconsolation and was now smiling and nodding. "Then come out to dinner with Iars and myself. Is that OK, Iars?"

"Of course," he said, smiling warmly at Veronica. Ted walked over to the reception area to sort out the spare room and I looked at Veronica, blushing to the roots and glowing in the heat of Iars' stare. There was every chance we wouldn't need that room after all.

What a bloody marvellous ending to a, frankly, fraught couple of days. At least I'd learned a few things. Such as, if a tent looks too small to be a tent, it probably isn't a tent, and always watch out for the cakes in Amsterdam, they do terribly unnerving things to you.

"Right, all sorted," said Ted, returning with a key.

"This is for you," he said to Veronica, and he put his arm round me. "You, my dear, will be staying in my room."

"Oh good." I let my head rest against his shoulder as we walked along. "I'm very happy about that."

BOOK THREE

Crazy Life of an Adorable Fat Girl

1. NO KNICKERS & A RED FACE

The door to the beauty salon made a welcoming sound as I opened it. You know the one I mean – kind of a tinkling sound – like you're entering a wonderful world of fairy magic.

Going to the beauticians is one of my favourite things in the whole world. All the gorgeous smells and the wildly over-made-up women in their nurse-like outfits drifting around talking in warm and calming voices; I think it's that combination of a woman who really loves her makeup (I mean *really* loves makeup – some of them wear so much of the stuff that their foundation enters the room five minutes before the rest of them), and a pseudo- scientific approach to the job, that makes them so appealing.

You know what I mean about the science – those uniforms they wear and all the talk of alpha hydroxides, illuminating particles and oxygen carrying molecules – I'm convinced every time that my life will be transformed by these women and their alluring potions and endless promises.

"This will make you look 10 years younger," a beautician with a sleepy smile will say.

"I will make your pores invisible and your wrinkles vanish."

"I will make you grow six inches taller and you'll become President of the United States of America."

OK, maybe not the last one, but you know what I mean? Who doesn't want to be in a world in which everyone is telling you they will make you look better? It's like the most perfect world ever.

The science is great, and very compelling – the beautician peers at your skin under a light so bright that it could light up the sky, staring at your skin with an intensity and determination normally reserved for nuclear fusion and brain surgery. It is as if the beauty technician is solving all the problems of the universe, you expect her to make a pronouncement about string theory or black holes, but she doesn't do that, she declares that you need a deluxe, rabbit ear facial or some other such tosh and your skin will be perfect. And you believe her. Well – I do. She could suggest absolutely anything to me at that stage and I'd be fine with it.

"We will spray essence of sea breeze onto your skin along with crushed crab heads." Fine.

"We'll cover your face in horse manure and dance around you, waving tea towels." Great.

"We'll put salt in your eyes and vinegar in your ears and sing the national anthem." Perfect.

Christ. It's so ridiculous.

And I'm absolutely sure every time that they cover my face in something like mashed up beetles' legs, sea moss and elephant semen that I'll emerge looking like Cameron Diaz. Because that's the thing about going to the beauticians – it's all about the hope. Hope of a prettier face, better skin, a tighter jaw line. It's all about the triumph of optimism over common sense.

I always think that this might be the one time that I leave after the treatments looking really different, really special. Alas, dear readers, I have to report that – to date – no treatment I've had has ever made the blindest bit of difference to the way I look. But I keep going. I keep turning up at the door with the tinkling sounds in the hope that it will work *this* time.

. . .

So, I went to the beauticians for a facial. They showed me through to a small 'consulting' room. I wasn't really sure whether I should get undressed and lie down on the bed, or wait for the beautician.

No one told me to get undressed, but clearly I knew I had to remove my top and I didn't want to look like a complete beauty amateur by waiting to be told everything, but – equally – I didn't want to be presumptuous. On balance I'd rather wait to be told, so I sat down and looked at the rows and rows of lotions, creams and sprays on the side, and enjoyed the strong smell of lavender sitting heavily in the air. The creams and lotions had alluring names – all of them promising to have a transformational effect upon the user. Whether you wanted to look younger, tighter, plumper or glossier, you could do so by simply picking up the relevant bottle and smearing the contents on your face.

I reached over and took one of the bottles. It said 'youth serum'. I couldn't resist it. I glanced at the door, then twisted the cap and attempted to put a couple drops of the serum into my hand. But I twisted the cap too much and tonnes of the bloody gloopy stuff came out. The liquid smelled like almonds but had the consistency of semen, which unnerved me a little. I rubbed the semen serum into my face. I'd just covered the right side of my face when the door opened and the beautician walked in. I quickly rubbed my hand against the towel on the bed next to me so she didn't know I'd been pinching her almond semen.

"Hello," she said, extending a very tiny, perfectly manicured hand. I reached out to shake it and watched in dismay at how much bigger my hand was than hers. Mine looked like a man's hand. A fat man's hand. Who on earth wants a fat man's hand? I bet even a fat man doesn't want a fat man's hand.

While we shook hands and exchanged polite greetings, I could feel the right side of my face tingling. It wasn't unpleasant – just a gentle feeling of warmth spreading through it. It felt nice. It felt like the serum was working – yay!

But no.

No.

What a disaster. I only had the serum on one side of my face. I became suddenly paranoid that one side of my face would look years younger than the other. I pictured half of me looking like Taylor Swift and the other half Theresa May. Not a good look.

The beautician was very exotic. If she were a smell she'd be cherry blossom and magnolia or lemon grass and pear (see how obsessed I was becoming with the smells? See how this place got to me?). She sat down and asked me what my concerns were about my skin. Really, I didn't know how much time she'd got, but I did have a lot of concerns. I began to reel them off...the redness around my nose, the puffiness around my eyes, the spots on my chin, the oily patch down the centre of my face. And the open pores. My God! My pores were so open I could store things in them. And wrinkles – don't forget the wrinkles!

"You're being very hard on yourself," she said in a foreign accent so strong that I could barely understand her. She sounded like she was from South Africa. "You have lovely skin and it will look even lovelier after the facial."

There we go...the promises, the hope, the optimism...

She had the most beautiful, caramel-coloured skin and gorgeous shiny black hair. There was more fat in my thumb than she had in her entire body.

"I'm going to go out of the room to let you get yourself sorted. Could you remove your knickers and lie back on the bed. Get yourself comfortable and I'll be back in a tick."

The lady moved to leave the room.

"Sorry, could you repeat that?" I said. She couldn't really want me to remove my knickers, could she?

"Just lie back on the bed," she said in her clipped accent. "Make yourself comfortable, and remember to remove your knickers. I'll be back in just a minute."

I knew I should run after her really, and ask her why on earth I had to remove my most intimate piece of clothing when I was having a facial. But I didn't, of course. In the same way that I don't scream "it's too bloody hot" if I'm at the hairdressers and they wash my hair in boiling water.

"Is the temperature OK?" the girl will ask, and even though my scalp is melting under her fingers, I say "yes, it's fine," knowing I'll have to go straight to A&E for a scalp transplant afterwards.

So, I took my knickers off and settled down on the bed with a small towel covering my embarrassment.

A few minutes later the lady came back in, smiled at me and took the towel off me.

"Whaaaaa…" she said, staring at me. "Why the hell did you remove your knickers?"

"You told me to," I insisted.

She backed away, towards the door, and looked at me as if I was completely mad.

"I said remove your necklace. Your necklace. Not your knickers."

"Ohhhh…"

I struggled back into my underwear and lay back on the bed. "Sorry," I muttered, as the smell of ylang-ylang and sandalwood filled the room. "I thought you said knickers. I wouldn't have taken them off otherwise. I'm not the sort of person who…"

"Sssshhh… just relax," she said as she massaged some sort of concoction that smelled like the earth into my face. "Relax and think about how beautiful you are going to look."

"OK." I sensed myself drifting away. "OK, I'll relax."

The facial was lovely. I almost fell asleep as she covered my face in a thick, heavy paste and said, to my delight, "I'm going to give you a massage while the face masque is doing its magic. She started to apply oil to her hands which she then began to massage into my legs and I began to really relax, but then I couldn't help but think about her tiny, delicate hands and how horrible it must be for her to have to massage my enormous, fat thighs. I wondered whether she was repulsed. She was so tiny, so small and delicate, I bet she'd never seen thighs as enormous as mine. As she massaged away I experienced an overwhelming urge to explain (lie) to her about why I was so fat.

Of course, the reason I'm overweight is because I eat too much, but that's not much of a story is it? So I told her all about my baby that had just been born. In fact, I told her I'd just had twins.

"How lovely," she said. "I'm so envious. I'd love to have a baby one day. Twins would be amazing. I'd love that more than anything in the world. How long ago did you have them?"

"Yesterday," I replied. (I know, I know, stupid answer, but I was under pressure and not thinking straight...what, with all the lavender and massaging and everything.)

"YESTERDAY?"

"Yep."

"My God. Really? That's amazing. I'll be really gentle with the massage," she said. "You probably shouldn't be here so soon afterwards."

"I'm fine. Honestly," I said, wishing I'd never embarked on this line of chatter. I really wanted her to carry on massaging me firmly. I love firm massages.

"Where are the twins now?"

"Sorry?"

"The twins...I wondered where they were."

"My friend has them outside."

"So sweet," said the beautiful therapist and I nodded in agreement in the darkness of the room. My imaginary babies were, indeed, very sweet.

"What are their names?"

"Pardon."

"I just wondered what their names were?" she asked.

Bugger.

"William and Kate," I said, without thinking.

"Oh. Nice. Very patriotic," she replied.

"Yes."

"OK, that's the end of the treatment. Has everything been OK for you?"

"Lovely," I mumbled. My skin was tingling like crazy, my shoulders were relaxed and I had two amazing imaginary babies named after a future King and Queen of England.

"I'm just going to turn the light up a little bit." She padded gently towards the door. "Don't get up quickly, take it easy, especially since you had your babies yesterday."

"Yeah, don't worry too much about the whole baby thing," I said. "Really, it was quite simple, no aggro."

"Holy fuck."

"What's the matter?" I asked as she stared at me, her face in her hands, her eyes wide as saucers.

"It's your face. Something weird has happened to your face – it's absolutely scarlet."

2. THE TROUBLE WITH TED

*I*t would have been a lie to say that my skin looked better after the facial; it would have been more accurate to describe me as looking like I'd been peeled and pickled. Yep, we'd need a whole new word for red. The beautician said that the 'blush' (BLUSH? I looked like I'd been boiled!) would go down within a few hours and I should make sure I didn't put any makeup on for 24 hours to get the full benefits of the treatment. So I was heading off to my friend Charlie's house looking like someone had rubbed a cheese grater against my face then sprinkled vinegar on top. Great! And I'd paid for it. And couldn't put any makeup on it to make it less angry-looking. Marvellous.

Charlie's my best, and oldest friend. She's known me forever and we used to do absolutely everything together when we were younger. She opened the door and gave me a huge hug, then she released me and glanced at my face before jumping back in horror. Her hands flew to her mouth.

"Good God, you look as if you've been attacked by wolves!" she said.

"No, no, I'm fine."

"Car crash?"

"No, honestly, I'm fine."

"Late onset meningitis?"

"No really, I just went for a facial today and I seem to have reacted to some of the products."

"Yeah, I'll say. *Reacted* is a bit of an understatement. Why's it so much worse on the right side of your face?"

"No idea."

"OK. And you're absolutely sure you don't need a doctor."

"Positive," I said. "The beautician wasn't at all alarmed and neither should I be."

This was a lie – the beautician was very alarmed; she screamed when she saw the colour I'd gone, and called for urgent assistance. The owner of the beauty salon came running down the corridor as fast as her silk Chinese slippers would allow her and threw cold water on my face. The red didn't fade. In fact it looked worse when wet. The two women looked at one another – completely out of options. "I think you need to go home and relax and it should fade," said one of them.

"Yes," said the other enthusiastically, as if her colleague had just solved the mysteries of the universe. "Sandra's right; it should fade. Just go and relax."

Despite their apparent conviction that going home (i.e. getting out of their salon before anyone saw me) was the best thing to do, they kept glancing one another in a way which screamed '*what the fuck do we do now?*'

"OK, well I guess the beauticians know what they're talking about," said Charlie. "Come on, come in." She swept her arm into the house for me to follow her inside, still staring at my face in a kind of squinty fashion as if she couldn't quite believe what she was seeing.

"How are you? I mean – besides the raw tomato face thing."

"I'm fine, really. I'm a lot better than I look."

"Christ, yes, I imagine you are. How is Ted?"

I was dreading this question. The truth was that Ted was great. He was kind and decent and honest and he loved me. But for some reason... I didn't know how...we were sort of drifting apart, and I found myself struggling to understand why. I didn't feel as madly in love with him as I used to be, and he was starting to annoy me quite a lot.

"Everything OK?" she asked. "I mean – Ted-wise?"

Charlie had heard everything she needed to know in my silence.

"Everything's not OK, is it?" she said. "Do you want to talk?"

"Everything's sort of fine," I replied. "I mean it's not *not fine* or anything."

"Sort of fine? Not *not fine?*"

"Sort of," I repeated.

"Glass of wine?"

"A large one would be great, thanks."

I followed her into the kitchen, jumping as I saw my bright red face in the hall mirror. I looked as if I was in a permanent state of extreme anger.

Charlie handed me a drink and we clinked glasses affectionately.

"So, things aren't going well with Ted?" she said.

"I don't know, Charlie. I'm not being evasive or anything, I just don't know. It's not that things aren't going well, it's just that I'm not really feeling it... Do you know what I mean? I don't know..."

"Have you spoken to Ted about this?" she asked. "Last time we had any sort of conversation about him you were ludicrously happy and mentally buying a wedding dress. What happened to change your mind?"

"I haven't spoken to Ted because I don't know what I'd say to him. I mean – it's not like I don't love him. And, yes, I know. I was obsessed with him...could think of nothing else. And he has done nothing wrong, and nothing has changed but I've sort of done this mental thing where I've switched off and gone off him. I don't know...it's nuts. Perhaps I'll just get over it."

· · ·

TED AND I HAVE BEEN SEEING EACH OTHER FOR ABOUT THREE MONTHS. We started going out together at the end of this Fat Club course that we both attended. Did I tell you I'm really fat? No? Well, I am, and so is he. We both lost some weight on the Fat Club course, but we both have loads to go. I need to shift a minimum of six more stone before I am anywhere near fighting weight. He's bigger – he reckons he is nine stone off his ideal weight. I know what you're thinking – that's a lot of weight – that's like two extra people we're carrying around with us. And you're right – but we are trying to lose the weight.

Since meeting on the Fat Club course we have carried on seeing one another all summer. We had an amazing time... We spent most nights of the week together and all weekend, in fact, we rarely went out. We seemed to spend all our time inside cuddling up together, watching TV or watching films. I think that if it weren't for Fat Club we'd have spent most of our time eating takeaways and drinking wine, because – let's be honest – that's a bloody marvellous way to pass the time, but we were good, and we cooked instead of getting takeaways. I even persuaded Ted to try salads, against his better judgement (believing green food was the stuff of the devil). I gave him an apple but when he bit into ithe made the most extraordinary face – full of pain and anguish. "There's no chocolate in mine," in the manner of a seven-year-old who's woken up on Christmas morning to no presents.

We had fun though – we had BBQs in the summer, sometimes inviting friends round, but usually with just the two if us. In fact – yes – it was just the two of us. Now I come to think of it we only talked of inviting other people round, but never actually got round to it, preferring to spend time alone, together. It was lovely – lying in the garden when it was warm, or in front of the TV later in the summer when things got colder. To be fair, we spent most of our time lying around. I wonder whether that was why the spark went. It's early November now and we were still lying around.

Not hard to see why things have gone a bit askew with me and Ted, is it? I suppose, fundamentally, it's quite boring to do the same thing every day. The other thing is I realise that I stopped making an effort. In the early days of the relationship I only had to think he might be coming round and I'd be thrown into a wild round of cleaning and organising the house, then shaving, moisturising, fake tanning and making myself up. It was exhausting. But fun. And seeing Ted's face when I opened the door always made it worthwhile. I guess somewhere along the line I stopped trying. I stopped dressing up for Ted. After all, what was the point? We were just lying on the sofa. I'd have a quick shower and brush my hair, but I was always in leggings and big, baggy t-shirts, not the lovely little 50s style dresses that I'd worn all the time when we first met and that Ted had loved so much.

I had to face the truth, as the summer had slipped into autumn, I'd stopped trying, and so had Ted. To be fair, this wasn't a one-way abandonment of the relationship. I think we were equally to blame. Ted would come round and let himself in, and I'd be sitting on the sofa, watching TV, or in the kitchen sorting things out. I'd make a cup of tea or (more likely) pour us a glass of wine and we'd both sit down on the sofa and that was our life. Gosh, when you look at it in black-and-white like that it's amazing we lasted so long.

The truth is that Ted and I had drifted into this space of existing together without really living or loving one another. It was a space that was – well – a bit empty.

"It sounds like you need to talk to him though," said Charlie. "Tell him you still love him but that you're concerned...you're not sure that things are as good as they were."

"But that'll just worry him. You know what he's like...he'll be in a real panic. What would I say? 'You are as lovely as ever, as considerate, kind and loving as you've ever been, but I just don't know whether we are really meant to be together, I no longer feel one bit excited when I think of you.'"

"No, maybe don't say that to him...that would be a bit harsh...but tell him that the two of you need to talk."

"Talk? All we do is bloody talk."

Charlie looked at me over the rim of her wine glass. It was quite a stern look that said 'don't fuck this up; Ted's a good guy.' And she was right. Ted was the all-time, ultimate good guy.

"Perhaps it's a passing thing." As I spoke I recalled the million butterflies I used to feel every time I saw him. I wished it was still like that. I wished that every time the phone rang I prayed it was him, but I didn't. And I didn't know whether that was because we were settling into a relationship in a really normal, healthy way, or whether this was the end of the infatuation period and the end of Ted and Mary. How does anyone know? He called me and chatted to me and I was distracted all the time…waiting for him to get off the phone so I could get on with things around the house. You don't have to be a relation-ship guru to see that that's not a good thing…not a good thing at all!

"I guess it's just become predictable and unexciting," I said. "That's not only his fault…it's my fault as well." As I spoke, my phone vibrated on the table and I knew straight away that it was Ted.

"You see – this is the problem – there's no mystery or excitement. I always know it's him," I said, turning over the phone to show Charlie what I meant, but instead of Ted's name on the screen, it was Dave's. More specifically it said *"Dishy Dave – hottie from downstairs."*

"Oh," said Charlie. "The hottie downstairs appears to be calling."

If I hadn't already been the colour of a hot chilli, I would have gone red. Why was Dave calling? Dishy Dave lived below me and I'll confess that I have had a few entanglements with him over the years. They'd never ended well for me, of course, because he was really, really gorgeous and had lots of other options. I knew he would prefer someone slimmer on his arm, but if he got desperate, he called me and I guess he thought that a fat female was better than no female. I'd had a few lively encounters with him as a result of this mindset, and I was very grateful every time (I have been known to thank him profusely during the course of the encounters, but let's not dwell on that now).

"So, are the problems with Ted anything to do with this Down-stairs Dave?" asked Charlie.

"No," I said, in all honesty. "Nothing to do with Double D." I hadn't been anywhere near the delicious man in the flat below me since I'd started seeing Ted. I hadn't wanted to.

I didn't know why Dave was ringing me, but it'd be something to do with him borrowing something, needing something or wanting me to keep an eye out for the latest glamorous blonde in his life. It wouldn't be to fix up an illicit meeting with me, sadly.

The times he'd called in the past had been notable for their lack of any actual interest in me.

There was one occasion when he called and said: "Tesco's are bringing my shopping, are you in to collect it?"

The honest answer was: "No, I'm not in."

Is that what I said to him?

Of course not. I wanted to be useful. I wanted to be the one to whom he turned when he needed anything. All in the vain hope that he'd realise one day, like the characters in every decent romantic comedy ever made, that the woman of his dreams was right beneath his nose all the time.

So, I said: "Sure, no problem. I'm here. I can help." Even though I wasn't, not by a long chalk – I was bloody miles away at Mum and Dad's house and had to leave mid-sentence with barely an explanation and break the land speed record to get home in time for the Tesco man.

"I'll call you later to explain," I'd shouted to Dad over my shoulder as I waddled at speed through the streets like a woman possessed. I'd flown towards the shared gate that led to mine and Dave's flats just as the Tesco lorry was driving off.

"Stop," I screeched, and it ground to a halt, reversing back into a parking space and beginning to unload bags of shopping. I signed for it all, found Dave's spare key under the bucket in the plants, and let myself into his filthy flat.

I put the shopping away (to be fair – it was mainly beer), then had a huge tidy up and sat down to wait for Dave's return. In my head he'd be so delighted that I'd stepped into the breach and not only brought in his shopping and put it away, but also tidied everything up, that he would instantly fall in love with me and ask me to marry him.

In the end, he didn't get home until 2am and had a glamorous blonde on his arm. I was a good 10 stone heavier than her (I really mean that – the woman can't have been more than eight stone for God's sake).

"What are you doing here?" asked Dave, quite angry, and not mentioning the vast amount of tidying up I'd done.

I slinked back to my flat and cried and ate a load of crisps.

Things like that happened a lot with me and Dave.

In fact, you could say that the only things that ever happened between me and Dave were like that.

So, on this occasion, I didn't take the call, and I switched my phone off.

"Right," I said to Charlie. "Let's talk about you; tell me what you've been up to."

"Well, it's funny you should ask," she said. "Did I tell you about Sam? The guy I met on Tinder."

"No." I poured more wine into my glass and went to put the bottle down when the glass was half-full.

"I strongly think that this is a large glass of wine sort of story," said Charlie, tipping so much wine into my glass that it was full to the brim and I could barely lift it. She filled her own glass.

"Well, he seemed nice…seemed normal," she said. "The picture on the site was good – he seemed to have hair and teeth and no facial tattoos…always a good start."

She told me how they'd met at the train station and he had a small bunch of flowers for her.

"A really nice touch," we agreed.

They went for a drink first and he mentioned his wife who died in a car crash 10 years earlier.

"Christ, how awful," I said. "How did she die?"

"She died when a car veered onto the pavement and hit her. She was taking their son to nursery at the time."

"Bloody hell, mate. That's awful."

"Yep. It's unbelievably awful. I felt so sorry for him. The trouble is, the whole date was all about his tragic story of lost-love. He didn't ask me anything about me. He didn't seem interested in who I was, or what I wanted, he was just glad to have someone to talk to about his late wife. Does that sound really harsh or selfish? It probably is, isn't it?"

"No, I know what you mean. It's a very sad story, but you still have to find a way to have a relationship. He has to ask something about your life, and not use you as free therapy. Tell me what happened afterwards. Did he take you home? Anything exciting happen?"

"We went for dinner, which was really nice – just in a pub in Esher. The food was amazing...really good. Then I invited him back to mine for coffee."

"Oooooo. Now it's starting to sound exciting." I bent over in an ungainly fashion to sip from the top of my wine glass because I couldn't pick the bloody thing up – there was too much wine in it.

"He said 'yes' he'd love to come in for coffee and would drive me home. I commented that I'd noticed he wasn't drinking anything and he said 'I haven't drunk a drop of alcohol since the moment that car hit my wife' and that was it – he was off again with all the detail...all the bloody gory detail about her blood-stained sweater and her going limp in his arms. It kind of killed the mood, to be honest. I didn't feel very sexy when he was moodily moaning about blood on the street.

"Then, just as I thought things couldn't get any worse, we get into the car, he turns the key and we head off in slightly the wrong direction. 'I think we're better off turning right here,' I say to him, pointing to the next junction.

"'No, let's go this way,' he insisted. 'I want to show you where the car hit her.'"

"Fuck," I said, downing the rest of my wine in one huge mouthful and struggling to swallow it without choking and spluttering.

"That's what I said. I asked him not to take me to where she bloody died, but he insisted. Honestly, Mary, hang on to Ted, he's a good guy and there are lots of nutters out there."

"Yes," I replied, rendered almost speechless by her tale. "Yes, you're probably right."

I got home that evening and forgot that my phone had been off. It's a weird thing when you're used to having it on all the time. So, I switched it on and waited patiently for all the beeps and rings to indicate that Ted had rung about 10 times, and left eight messages.

Silence.

I checked through the message folder: nothing.
I rang the answer phone: nothing.
Oh.
Ted hadn't phoned.
I wasn't expecting that.

3. HAS HIS PHONE BROKEN OR SOMETHING?

No call from Ted in the morning. Nothing at all.

I didn't care, to be honest. The relationship was dying, so I guessed it was best that he had lost interest. But I wondered why he'd lost interest. I checked the phone again. No missed call. Perhaps my phone was broken? I rang myself from my landline and the mobile began singing in front of me. It was working OK. I texted myself. Yep – the text came bouncing through.

Bugger.

Whatever. I didn't care.

Except…I kind of, sort of, did care…just a little bit. This was weird. I did like him, and I wanted him to like me. I didn't want him pulling away…that wasn't in the plan at all.

I suppose the good news in it all was that I'd be seeing Ted every Tuesday night from now on at Fat Club, because it re-started that evening. Yay! The second course.

I was quite excited that it was starting up again. I knew it didn't say much for my social life that I was really thrilled to be spending an evening talking about calories and self-control, but I'd made loads of great friends on the first course (including Ted) and it would be nice to catch up with everyone again. Also I was really hoping I could get back into the weight losing groove, and shed a couple more stone.

So, when evening descended on Cobham I was on the bus and heading to the crumbling community centre that passed as home for Fat Club. I got a little shiver of familiarity as I approached. I remembered walking in on the first day and thinking that this really wasn't for me, but then – by the end of the course – I was totally sold on it. Suddenly my mind was flooded with memories of meeting Ted here. He was so loveable, kind and gorgeous. Fat, of course, or why else would he have been there? And not conventionally good-looking at all – kind of half-shy, half wildly over-confident. Sometimes he would smile at me and nudge me quietly when no one was looking and I'd feel a shiver of excitement run through me. God, it's always so amazing at the beginning of a relationship, isn't it? Pity so many of them turn to shit after a few months.

As well as seeing Ted at Fat Club, I'd also see the other friends I'd made, because they were all coming back for this second course. The first course had all been about losing weight – this one was about losing *more* weight. Guess what the next course was called? 'Losing *even* more weight.' Not sure what would happen after that: 'Losing so much weight it's unbelievable', 'Coping with being too thin'? I don't know. All I did know was that the first course worked like a dream – I felt happier, more confident and – crucially! – thinner after it, so I was going in again.

I walked inside, and saw I was the third person to arrive. Liz, the course leader, was in the room, standing at the front, sorting out her notes, while Janice chatted away to her.

"And then he killed his wife and ran off with the butcher's son!" she was saying. "Can you believe that?"

"Blimey," I said. "You don't half socialise with some colourful characters."

"No, not my social life," she said. "This is the plot of the book that Liz told me to read."

"That's a relief." I waddled over to Janice and gave her a kiss on the cheek. "I was worried about you for a minute then."

"Hi, Liz, are you OK?" I kissed her on the cheek as well. "What have you got planned for us then? Anything weird or complicated?"

"Nothing weird," said Liz. "We'll just be doing more of what we did on the first course, but probing; trying to find out why people are eating too much, why it's become a crutch and leaning on each other for moral support."

"OK – sounds good," I said. "I never thought I'd say this but I've missed the regular group meetings, it'll be really nice to get into them again."

"That's good to hear," said Liz. "Most people come back for the second course after they've been successful on the first one, and they always say it's because they find it such a supportive environment, and find they miss it when the first course stops."

"Yep, that's me." I watched Liz as she continued to remove things from her large bag. She pulled out a set of weighing scales.

"What the fuck?" I said.

"You're not going to bloody weigh us?" added Janice.

"That's the spirit," said Liz, the sarcasm dripping off every word. "Be enthusiastic and encouraging."

"But – they are weighing scales," I pointed out. "Weighing scales! I'd be less terrified if you had pulled out a gun."

"You're not going to weigh us?" said Janice.

"No, of course not."

"Then why would you have weighing scales?"

Honestly, bringing out weighing scales at a Fat Club is like bringing out a bomb or something. I noticed that Janice had physically recoiled from the sight of it.

"Can you put it away," she said. "You're making me feel queasy."

"Don't be silly now, ladies," said Liz, shaking her head, pushing her hand into her bag and pulling out a tape measure.

"Whooooah. And you can put that back from where you got it as well," said Janice.

"I'm not going to use them to measure you with, if that's what you're worried about."

"That's what I'm very worried about," said Janice. "Why would you have them if you weren't going to use them on us?"

"Yes," I added in a slightly trembling voice, unable to take my eyes off the scales.

"Oh, for goodness' sake." Liz put them back in her bag. "You two are ridiculous. You've both done so well and lost so much weight. Isn't it time to be proud of how much you weigh?"

"Proud?" I said. "I'm six bloody stone overweight, proud is certainly not how I'm feeling."

It's one thing discussing our difficulties with food, and trying to learn to readjust and alter our mindsets, but it's quite another thing to be humiliated publicly. If people knew how much I weighed they'd be astonished I was able to walk properly without my legs breaking beneath me.

"Hi," I said as Veronica walked into the room and saw us all staring at Liz as she stuffed the scales and tape measure into her bag.

"Oooo...what are they for? I'm not being weighed, not for anyone."

"Not another one," said Liz. "They're not for weighing."

"What on earth are they for then?" asked Veronica.

Liz continued to put the scales into her bag, and to remove notes, books and what looked like a skipping rope.

"I'm not skipping either – you can forget about that. With boobs this size I'd knock myself out."

"Will you lot stop worrying. Nothing terrible is going to happen. You're not going to have to do anything. These are for my next class – not for you. I was just checking that I have everything I need. So you can all just relax."

"I CAN'T RELAX WITH THAT SKIPPING ROPE ON THE TABLE...IT'S terrifying. I feel like I'm back in school and am not invited to join in the skipping games."

"Bloody hell, ladies – you're hard work tonight." Liz put the skipping rope back into the bag with the scales and tape measure. She looked up. "Happy now?"

"Much happier," said Veronica with a smile. I'd forgotten how attractive Veronica is. She was a former model with the loveliest face ever – like a doll's. She had porcelain skin...kind of like Sophie Dahl used to look before she lost all that weight and let us all down. Veronica's big, but she was in proportion and very curvy...I mean *very*. Huge big breasts that probably had their own postcode and a big squishy bottom that I'm sure men adored.

She was a real sweetie but I confess that I didn't like her at first. She was quite stand-offish and it seemed like she wanted to tell everyone that she used to be a model all the time, like we were supposed to treat her differently or something. Perhaps I was jealous? I don't know, but I didn't really want to be around her, then – after the end of the first course she was very sweet to me, and we ended up going shopping together and became friends. Now I really like her. She told me about how she'd always wanted to be a model and was devastated when it ended. She felt like a complete failure and felt like she wasn't qualified to do anything else. I realised she kept saying that she used to be a model because she felt that was all she had going for her. Far from showing off, she was desperately insecure and trying to hide the insecurity. I like her a lot and I'm sure she'll always be a friend.

"You OK, gorgeous?" she said.

"I'm fine, thanks," I said.

She sat next to me so I had Janice one side and Veronica the other. For a fleeting moment I thought to myself that I should ask her to move so Ted could sit next to me. But then I remembered that Ted hadn't called or texted or made any effort to get in touch with me for two days. TWO DAYS! He was dead to me. I was glad to be in the middle of a Janice and Veronica sandwich.

"Where's Ted?" asked Veronica, as if she could read my mind.

"He's not here yet." I tried to sound as neutral and unbothered as possible. "I'm sure he'll be here soon."

"Hello there," came a voice from the doorway – it was Phil and his wife. They were both elderly, and they were the only people I didn't really get to know on the last course. They sat together, quietly and didn't chat to us. When it was time for them to speak, they stood up and told their life stories, but always together (it was all kind of sweet in a way, but it meant that none of the rest of us got close to them, so they were a bit of a closed shop). They didn't join in any of our post-session drinks, and were quiet during the sessions themselves. All I knew about them was that they were both called Phil: Philippa and Philip, known as the Phils. They said that at their work (because not only did they have the same name, they also worked in the same place) they were known as the Fat Phils. I laughed out loud when she said that, but the look on Philippa's face told me that it wasn't a laughing matter. In fact it was a major bone of contention and she absolutely hated that they were known in such derogatory terms.

I was determined to make friends with them on this course, and spend a bit of time getting to know them. They seemed like nice people and it was a shame that they weren't properly part of the group simply because they arrived in a couple and not on their own like the rest of us. I was determined to pull them into the centre of our little group. I'd be the club's social secretary.

The masculine Phil was resplendent in a large overcoat and the feminine Phil sported a sturdy-looking winter coat in a kind of boiled wool, dyed olive green. Possibly the most unflattering coat ever made. She was wearing brown tights and lace-up brown shoes exactly the same colour so that her legs blended seamlessly into her feet – like she'd got hooves. The shoes were deeply unattractive – the type of orthopaedic shoes that might be given to a child with an unfortunate birth condition that has resulted in one leg growing longer than the other.

I walked over to them in my new role as self-appointed social secretary. Veronica watched me go with a quizzical look on her face.

"Hello, we never really got to know each other on the last course," I said.

"No," said Phil, in a way which made it sound as if that was entirely by design, and he was eager to avoid us getting to know one another on this one.

"I'm Mary," I said, smiling broadly.

"You have lipstick on your teeth, Mary," said Philippa. For Christ's sake, could she not just smile and shake my hand? I was trying my hardest here.

I rubbed my tongue across my front teeth.

"We should all make more of an effort to get to know each other this time," I said, and Philippa looked quite terrified. "I mean – we hardly spoke to one another on the last course...why don't you come out for a drink with us one night?"

"We don't drink," said Phil.

"Well, come and have a Coke or coffee or something?" I tried.

"I don't think so," he said. "Thanks for asking."

I turned round to return to my seat and walked straight into Janice. "I don't want to be social secretary any longer," I told her. "The job's yours."

As I sat down I was still running my tongue along the front of my teeth to make sure the lipstick had all gone. This is the problem with bright red lipstick – if it gets anywhere but your lips it looks bloody awful...collars, sleeves and especially teeth.

I decided on red lips today to match my red dress. I was wearing it to show Ted what he was missing. He liked me in red. I liked me in red. So I was slightly confused as to why I'd been wearing grey leggings and t-shirts all summer. It was quite a figure-hugging dress for me and I felt ever so slightly self-conscious, but I knew this was a dress that Ted really liked, and even though I didn't care a damn about him and, frankly, didn't care whether he turned up or not that night, I wanted him to be impressed if he did.

Oh God, here he is.

I subconsciously tidied my hair as I saw him appear through the door. My stomach was in knots...probably because of the food I'd eatenearlier. I'd made a spicy chicken saladNot the best decision in the world for someone who's rubbish when it comes to eating spicy foods. Then I noticed. He was wearing the blue jumper I'd given him. Ahhhh, he looked really, really nice. God, I'd missed him. Why had I decided I didn't like him any more? I did like him...I mean – really liked him – look at him – he was just lovely.

Ted walked over towards me and I didn't know what to do. We'd been ignoring each other and I didn't quite know why. I had butterflies in my stomach and I felt madly self-conscious. I looked down and started pretending to dig into my bag for something. When I looked up, he had gone over to talk to Liz, and was kissing her on both cheeks and asking her about the course. Fuck. Why was I behaving like such an idiot?

Ted looked good, I had to admit that. He'd taken the jumper off and you could see clearly that, in common with most of us, he'd lost a few stone since the first course and it really suited him. He had jeans on with the shirt tucked into them, and while no one could accuse him of being too thin, I could remember the days when he would only wear the baggiest of shirts, and they always hung outside his jeans. He used to walk around with a look of desperate embarrassment at his own existence. That had turned to mild confidence. He looked like a man who was comfortable in his skin. It's amazing what losing weight can do for a person.

It was so great to see everyone back in the room where we'd first met; there was a real familiarity, warmth and happiness in being with these people with whom I'd been through so much.

We'd all lost weight since the last course, but more importantly than that, we'd all realised why we were eating so much. We'd all listened to the lectures and heard each other's stories. We understood that we had convinced ourselves, somewhere deep down, that eating was going to make us feel better, feel loved, or feel so full that we wouldn't worry any more about the problems that seemed to haunt us like ghosts in the night.

Through my eating I was literally trying to smother all the problems I had. The great irony for me was the discovery that the 'problems' I had were largely related to my self-esteem, and that self-esteem hinged on what I looked like. So – for heaven's sake – every time I ate to hide my problems, I was making my problems worse because I felt more unattractive to myself as I got bigger, which ate away at my diminishing self-esteem.

Coming onto the first course helped me recognise that, and put a stop to it. I did some sort of psychological switch whereby I knew I wasn't eating because I was hungry – I was eating to make myself feel good, and I stopped it. I did other things that made me feel good – things like walking and swimming, and the weight started to come off. The more it came off, the happier I felt, and the less inclined I was to eat

I hadn't been perfect, and I had strayed from the straight and narrow at times, which was why I'd been eager for the class to start up again, but I'd been pretty good, all in all. Sure, I could eat a packet of biscuits in one sitting, and if you saw me wolf down a bag of chips you'd think that my psychological problems were as bad as ever, but they're weren't. I'd eat and eat and eat and then I'd have a moment of lucidity when I realised what I was doing and I'd stop. I'd never had those feelings of lucidity before. To be honest, I never stopped until I started crying or started feeling sick. Since the first course I could still eat loads and loads but then I'd think 'what the hell are you doing, woman?' and I'd stop. And I didn't do it again the next day and the day after.

4. THE NEW GIRL AT FAT CLUB

"Just waiting for one more person," said Liz, with a gentle shrug of her shoulders and a warm smile. That woman had been such a support to me since the last course ended: phoning up to keep me on track, and making sure she checked in with me from time to time, just to make sure I was OK.

"No, we're all here," I said, looking around the room and smiling at everyone except Ted. I still couldn't look at him. He made me feel all nervous and jittery and I was terrified about the fact that he didn't call me or anything.

Why didn't he call me? He was supposed to like me. People who like you, call you.

He half-smiled at me, then sucked the smile in as I looked away, and I wished immediately that I hadn't looked away. Why the hell did I look away? And why the hell didn't he just come over and say hello, or talk to me, or behave like any half-normal human being would?

"Ah, but we're not all here," said Liz. "Because we have a newcomer who will be turning up for the session tonight…"

Everyone in the room looked at Liz. This was most unwelcome news. We'd become such a tight-knit group, sharing details of our issues with food and stories about failed weight loss in unabandoned fashion. We trusted each other and felt comfortable with each other. We'd delved deep into our psyches and shared information with the group that was personal, sad and touching. There had been tears, smiles and anguish, as we'd talked about the deaths of those close to us and how they sent us spiralling into anguish and overeating. I felt I knew more about some of the people in that room and what they'd been through than I knew about members of my own family. How could someone new be joining us?

The door at the back of the hall opened and in walked a large woman (of course...she'd hardly be here if she was Kylie Minogue size). She was dressed beautifully, in a pair of cut-off jeans and an off-the-shoulder red and white polka dot top. She looked like she ought to be in St Tropez or something with her incredible suntan and lashings of red lipstick. I looked down at my outfit and suddenly I felt dowdy. Her red was brighter and her lips were like glistening cherries. I was not the brightest, most eye-catching person in the room any more and it disturbed me more than it should.

"I'm Michella," she said with a massive smile that stretched right across her face.

I hated that she was so pretty, but most of all I hated that she seemed so nice with it.

"Come and sit here," said Ted with a smile, indicating the seat next to him.

What?

Fuck. No.

She ran her hand through her blonde hair. It was a shade or two lighter than mine which made me really cross. I wanted to be the brightest blonde in the room. I love having blonde hair. I've always loved it.

I remembered being at school, and sitting on the benches at the back as a fifth former, slightly elevated from the rest of the children and looking down onto the heads in front of me. All the heads were shades of brown. Sure there was the occasional blonde head but it was mainly brown. Any blonde head would stand out like ripe corn in a muddy field and I vowed that I would always be blonde.

I remembered when I first dyed my hair, my mum and dad were really cross, but I loved it... I thought I look like a movie star. I thought I looked like my Barbie that I'd played with as a little girl. I thought I looked like a woman should look – bright, pretty and alluring but with an edge of vulnerability. I thought I looked fantastic and I've been dyeing my hair ever since. In some ways, I was quite envious of people like Janice with her mousey hair, and the fact that she felt no compunction to hide her natural state. I was all about hiding mine. I didn't want to be natural and 'myself' on the outside. If you are a mouse inside, I think you feel drawn to becoming a peacock on the outside.

"Hello, nice to meet you," she said to me, having thoroughly ingratiated herself with my boyfriend.

"I'm Mary," I said, ignoring the way Ted was smiling at me. I was sure Ted's smile was screaming: "Look, look – a pretty girl. You have been replaced..." And no – I wasn't being paranoid.

"Have you been on a sunbed?" she asked.

"No," I replied. Most of the redness had gone out of my skin following my disastrous beauty treatment, but clearly not all of it.

"Oh, an allergy of some kind?"

"No."

"A rash?"

"No."

For God's sake, woman. Let it go, will you.

"OK, let's get started," said Liz, rising to her feet and smiling at us. "You'll have noticed that we have a new girl in our midst..."

Yes, we've all noticed, I thought to myself. There was nothing interesting about a new girl turning up, in fact it was a positive distraction. I wanted to just get on with the session and not obsess about someone new being here. But – no – of course they couldn't do that. We all had to get to know this glamorous young creature who'd crawled into our little group. To make it all worse, Michella was invited to go straight to the front of the room and give a small talk to us.

I looked at the way she walked…it was positively sick-making. Silly cow with her wiggly hips and big bottom. No one's impressed, love. No one's impressed.

"Hello, my name is Michella," she said, running a hand through her blonde hair and pushing it back over her shoulder. She was very pretty – disturbingly so. I was sure she was exactly Ted's type. Let's be honest, she looked like a prettier, younger version of me. Bitch.

"People call me 'Mich' for short," she said, looking around the room with big blue eyes framed by long eyelashes that I was sure she kept fluttering in the direction of my boyfriend. Did she really need to do that?

"OK, where do I start? I'm really overweight, as you can see. I look horrible, and I feel horrible, and I'd go as far as to say that a lot of the time I really hate myself. I want to do something about it, but for some reason I don't seem able to sort my head out and I sabotage myself every time I try to lose weight. I thought that by being in a supportive environment like this I might be able to change the way I am, and eventually lose weight. You all seem really nice, so that's a really good start!"

She looked around the room, desperate for encouragement, and I knew it was really evil, but I was silently praying that no one offered her any.

"We're all here for you," said Ted, kindly, and I felt like punching him.

"Yes," added Janice. "We look after each other in this group." I feared I might explode with anger. She was such a traitor.

"I know why and when I started putting on weight – it's not a very happy story, but I feel I ought to tell you, so you fully understand me and what I've been through."

Oh great. This was obviously going to take bloody hours.

"I had a twin sister called Emily," she said, pausing for a moment before giving a faint laugh to cover up the fact that she was getting emotional. "Phew. I knew it was going to be difficult to tell you about this.

"Anyway, Emily got ill when we were young. She had leukaemia, aged just 12, I remember it like it was yesterday; like it was this morning; like it was two minutes ago. I remember it all so clearly, in fact it's like she's still here with me now, like she'll walk in any moment and hug me and we'll carry on playing with our dolls and everything will be OK. But it won't, because the leukaemia took her away from me. We can't talk about boys any more, or moan at each other for stealing each other's clothes or dance to our favourite pop music. We can't do any of it. She died and I just couldn't cope, and I suppose – looking back – I was left on my own to cope because my parents were struggling too. They comforted each other, they cried together and screamed together and threw themselves into the organisation of the funeral and into setting up a charitable foundation. Me? I just ate."

Michella burst into tears, holding her side and sobbing with all her heart. I did feel sorry for her – I'm not that callous. It must be unbelievably hard to lose a twin. I mean – to lose a sister would be beyond awful, but a twin sister…that must be so much worse.

"I'm sorry, I'm really sorry, I thought it was important to talk through this because I think that's why I eat so much – because the pain is killing me and I still try to bury it under food. Even talking to you today has made me think that now I could really do with a big cream cake!"

Everybody laughed and there were more mutterings of support, and people telling her how incredibly brave she was.

Michella then went on to describe the painful death of her sister. The two of them played together until the day before she died. She spoke about how brave her sister was, never complaining, always enthusiastic and talking about the future. "She must have known that she wouldn't be here to enjoy so many of the things we spoke about, but she continued to plan and to talk about the future, and we wrote to *Top of the Pops* and said we wanted to be in the audience, and we wrote to our favourite pop stars and asked them for autographs, and in none of the letters she sent did she mention she was ill. It was like she didn't want it to affect anything. When she died, it felt that everything was pointless. The only thing that made me happy was food. The weight piled on and I didn't care, I'd get exhausted running for the bus and it didn't bother me in the least. Now, though, it does. I lost my sister half a lifetime ago, and I need to start living again. For her. She's not here to enjoy life, so I need to enjoy it doubly as much... I need to start enjoying life for her as well as for me."

When she finished, there was a huge round of applause and a standing ovation, and she stood in the middle of it all just beaming.

The rest of us went up one by one and gave short talks about what we'd done since the last course. I kept mine brief. I just talked about my weight and my eating. Then Ted went up.

"It's been the best few months ever," he told everyone. "Because I've spent so much of it with Mary."

I looked up, stunned.

"She's changed my life. I'm a better man when I'm with her."

I could feel myself staring vacantly at Ted as he spoke. Everyone was staring at me, this was surreal. Ted came up to me afterwards and wrapped his arms around me.

"I know you've been busy so we haven't been able to see much of each other, but I absolutely adore you and I miss you," he said.

"I thought you'd gone off me," I replied. "When you didn't text me last night, I thought you didn't want to go out with me."

"I was giving you space," he said. "I thought you wanted some head space. I thought I was doing the right thing."

"Yes," I said. "You were. I'm an idiot."

"Are you coming for a drink?" he said, as Liz packed her stuff away and told us she'd see us next week.

"Yes." I smiled up at him. He put his arm round me.

"And are you?" he asked Mich.

"I'd love to," she said cheerily, taking his other arm in a way which REALLY annoyed me.

"Come on, you handsome hunk," she said to Ted, and I could feel my blood pressure rising. Why did she annoy me so much? She was so flirty, it was bloody horrible.

We got to the pub and she was no better, asking Ted to choose a drink for her and stroking his hair while he did. To his credit, he looked uncomfortable with all the attention, but he didn't push her away. He didn't tell her it was inappropriate.

Eventually I couldn't do it any longer. "Right, I'm off," I said to a bewildered-looking Ted, and I stomped out of the pub without saying goodbye to anyone else. I shuffled out into the cold night air and hid around the corner from Ted who had followed me. I didn't know why I'd done this. Even I was confused at the way I was behaving. If I'd gone and spoken to Ted and told him I wanted to go home, he'd have taken me. And that would have been all my problems solved – I'd get him to myself and away from Michella. Bingo! But for some reason I couldn't bring myself to make life easy. I couldn't bring myself to run into his arms and make everything right. I didn't know why. Something was stopping me.

After a while, Ted went back into the pub and I stepped out of my hiding place and got on the bus home. All I could think about was eating. It was the ONLY thought in my mind. I got off the bus right by the off-licence, Tesco's and the chip shop – one next to the other: an unholy triumvirate of temptation.

I stood outside the chip shop looking mournfully through the window and feeling anger and frustration rising inside me. I wanted to go in there and buy about six packets of saveloy and chips with a side portion of curry sauce, then I wanted to buy bread and butter and wine, and I wanted to swig the wine from the bottle without pouring it into a glass.

The thought of it all thrilled me. The more I could eat and drink, the more I would bury all the anger and frustration inside me. I stood in the cold night air for what seemed like hours, just smelling the vinegar. I wasn't hungry and the smell wasn't making me think 'ooooo...delicious', the smell was making me think 'ooo...here is something that I can use to make myself feel better...here is something that will make the pain go away...not for long, but for a short while, and right now any break from my mad, whirring thoughts will be good.'

"Can I help you, Mary?" asked the lady inside.

Oh God.

The fact that she knew my name made me feel like I'd been shot. How could the lady in the chip shop know my name?

"Everything OK?" she asked.

"Yes," I said, retreating from the alluring smells and warmth. "Everything's fine."

And I knew what I had to do. I had to reach out for help. I pulled my phone out of my pocket. There were lots of missed calls from Ted, and I felt a low pain deep inside me when I saw his name on the screen. Tears started pouring from my eyes as I dialled Liz's number. She should have finished her next class by now. Relief flooded through me when she answered on the second ring.

"Are you alright?" she asked.

"No," I said, bursting into tears. "I feel terrible, I'm messing everything up. I'm standing outside the chip shop and I'm dying to go in, I just want to eat. I've ruined my relationship with Ted and I don't know why. Everything in my life feels completely out of control."

"Well, that's simply not true, is it?" said Liz, calmly. "Everything in your life is not out of control because instead of having chips you rang me. Instead of falling into food as the answer, you reached out, and I'm going to try and help you. I want you to walk back to your flat, go inside, put the kettle on and wait for me to arrive. We're not going to let you sabotage this lovely relationship you've got, and we're not going to let you sabotage your weight loss campaign – we're going to talk this through and sort it out, OK?"

"Yes," I muttered.

"You're just feeling insecure and unworthy, and you're pushing Ted away because your self-esteem is struggling. I could see it all over you tonight. We can sort this out. Go and put the kettle on."

"Thank you," I said, all tears and snot. "Thank you so much."

5. LIZ IS MY HERO

"ight, young lady: first question – did you get chips?"

"No," I said, in all honesty. I did buy two bottles of wine, just in case, but she didn't ask me about wine, so I kept that to myself.

"Well done, lovely," she said, giving me a huge hug. "I'm very proud of you."

"I don't feel very proud of myself." I burst into tears again. "I've been treating Ted appallingly and I just don't know why. What's wrong with me? He's the nicest guy ever. I'm such a fucking idiot, I'm such a loser. Why am I doing this? Look at the state of me? It's not as if men are queuing up to be with me. For God's sake – I'm ridiculous. I don't deserve him."

While I collapsed in floods of tears, Liz stroked my back gently.

"Do you want me to tell you what I think is going on?" she said.

"Yes please," I spluttered through a veil of tears.

"Right. Well, I think all the answers to every question you have are tucked away in what you've just said."

"Are they?"

"Yes, look, what drove you to eat a lot in the first place were your emotional issues. You felt you weren't worthy, you felt criticised by your parents and deeply unloved as a child, am I right?"

"Yes," I said. Those were certainly all the reasons for my overeating that we identified on the first course.

"Now, what we've learned on the course so far is that eating to excess is not the answer. Eating gives you temporary reprieve from your feelings, but it doesn't change them, so there's no point in stuffing yourself full of food in order to bury feelings – the feelings will still be there and you'll get fatter and fatter."

"Yes, I know, and I've been good – I had a breakthrough on the course and learned to completely accept that eating doesn't change anything when it comes to feelings and emotions."

"You've been amazing," confirmed Liz. "Now, let's just think about those feelings and emotions that are all churned up because of what you went through as a child. They are still there. You are learning to live with them, and learning not to suppress them with food, but they haven't gone anywhere. So, what happens is, from time to time, they get the better of you – they rear up and they attack you as sudden panic, anger, frustration or plain madness. I'm the same. I can act in the most obscure of ways when my emotions kick off, or when someone says something, however innocent and benign it may appear on the outside, but for some reason it starts something off in me and I just fall into a whirlwind of confused emotions. Unfortunately, when you feel like that, you often take it out on the person closest to you…as you have…with Ted."

"Yes," I said, feeling calmer all the time at the news that I wasn't bonkers, and what I was going through was something that even Liz herself had struggled with.

"It might be worth talking to someone," she said.

"I'm talking to you."

"No, I mean a psychiatrist…someone trained properly to help you."

"Is that expensive?" I asked. It certainly sounded like it would be an expensive thing to do.

"No, if you go through your GP, you'll get it on the NHS. You need to be really clear with the GP about how bad you're feeling. Tell him or her everything, and you'll get a referral and should see someone soon," she said. "In the meantime, I want you to follow these instructions if you feel down, concerned or worried." She placed a list of actions to follow on the edge of my desk. "They will help."

"Thank you," I said to Liz, giving her a big hug. "You've really helped."

I didn't know whether it was the process of talking that helped me, or whether something Liz said registered with me, but I felt better – much better. I could go and get help. Everything would be OK.

I walked over to the fridge and poured myself a large glass of wine to celebrate. Everything was going to be OK.

6. BUGGER, BUGGER, BUGGER

*W*ell, that didn't go brilliantly. It was hard, in many ways, to work out how it could have gone worse. You know that one glass of wine I had after Liz had left? It turned into two. Yes, I know what you're thinking – two glasses is OK – stop worrying.

Mmmm... I wish!

I had two bloody bottles.

Two bottles.

Fuck.

It was now 5am and I was wide-awake and struggling with the worst hangover in the world. My head was pounding inside my skull, so much so that I didn't want to lift it off the pillow because I was worried that my brain might literally burst through and bounce across the room. I had to move because I knew I had to get some water or I'd get worse and worse and never get back to sleep again.

OK, here we go... I stepped out of bed and saw my phone lying on the bedside table.

Oh shit. That was when I remembered.

I texted Ted last night. Shit. Shit shit shit. Why did I think it was a good idea to text anyone at 1am? Why didn't I just go to sleep after Liz left? I felt great then – energised and happy. But for some reason I started drinking, and the drinking made the emotions darker and I drank more to cover them… I did everything that I knew I wasn't supposed to do.

I picked up my phone, and the text was there – sitting on the screen, looking up at me:

"What the fuck am in wine and drinking and that stupid woman Michella fuck her. Am in wine."

Oh God. Really? I was sure I used to have some sort of self-preservation that kicked in when I was drunk and stopped me from sending texts like that. When I was young I'd go out to nightclubs and get blind drunk with my friends, but still somehow return home in one piece and without sending absurd texts to men.

I sat down at my desk and looked forlornly at the computer, open on Ted's Facebook page. Oh God. I hadn't messaged him through Facebook as well, had I? I clicked onto Facebook messenger…thankfully I hadn't attempted to contact him. I came back out onto his page.

Fucking wonderful.

It said: "Ted is now friends with Michella Bootle."

Great! He'd befriended her on Facebook.

And that was it. I was off again…my mind spinning and my stomach churning.

I bet he walked her home after the drink last night, and went in for coffee, and snuggled up on the sofa, and perhaps even had sex. I bet they did have sex. I bet it was better sex than he'd ever had with me. Then he climbed out of her bed and headed home, and immediately befriended her on Facebook.

I decided that I, too, would befriend Michella on Facebook. You know what they say – keep your friends close and your enemies closer. Michella was about the biggest enemy a woman could ever have. I would keep her close.

I sent her a friend request, and it gave me the option to add a message, so I tapped out a friendly note: "Hi Mich, it was lovely to meet you last night. I'm really sorry I had to rush off but I felt unwell. I hope you had a good time and look forward to seeing you next week."

Then I stared at the screen like a woman demented. I hit refresh several times. Why wasn't she responding? I decided it must have been because she was in bed with Ted. They were in bed together at that very moment. I carried on hitting refresh in a maniacal fashion. Then I saw the piece of paper that Liz left me with last night, and I followed her instructions...

1. Breathe deeply
2. Put two feet firmly on the floor
3. Clear your mind
4. Think about the earth beneath you and the walls in front of you...ground yourself
5. Repeat to yourself that this will pass...everything will be OK

"EVERYTHING WILL BE OK," I SAID. "EVERYTHING WILL BE OK." I repeated this until my eyes were closing and my bed was calling. I staggered through the apartment and flopped onto my bed, disgusted with Ted and disgusted with Michella, but calmer...much calmer.

By the time I woke up in the morning, there was a message from Michella: "Lovely to be friends on Facebook, Mary. Thanks so much for the invitation. I only stayed for one drink last night, then my boyfriend picked me up. Really looking forward to seeing you next week... Ted was telling me how madly in love with you he is. X"

Fuck, fuck, fuck.

7. MAKING IT ALL RIGHT AGAIN

"*I*'m sorry."

Little words that should be easy to say, but are so hard in practice.

I looked into the mirror and said the words again: "I'm sorry."

Christ, now all I had to do was say them to Ted. This was going to be much harder than I thought it would.

I picked up my phone and started pacing around the room. "Come on, Mary – you can do this," I said to myself in the manner of a boxer, revving himself up for the fight of his life. "You can do it, girl. You can do it."

Ah, but I couldn't. I put the phone down.

Oh God, this was so crazy. This man meant the world to me, why couldn't I just pick up the phone and talk to him? Why couldn't I stop this madness? I wanted to be with him. But I couldn't phone him – I was too scared. Too scared he might dump me as soon as he heard my voice.

Text. That was what I'd do – I'd send a text.

I knew that was wimpy but it was better than doing nothing, and I really wanted to get a message through to him sooner rather than later.

"I'm sorry," I typed into the phone, and hit send before I could change my mind.

"What are you sorry for?" he replied straight away.

"I'm sorry for everything. I'm sorry I have been so horrible to you, I'm sorry I rushed out last night, I'm sorry for sending a horrible text. I'm really, really sorry. Ted – I'm sorry you're not here in my arms right now. I'm just sorry."

Tears were in my eyes as I hit the send button.

"Are you at home?" he texted back.

"Yes," I replied.

"I'm on my way, if that's OK," he replied.

"Yes, of course it is!" I texted back, and it felt like the greatest day ever.

I sat back and smiled to myself. Ted was coming over. Then I realised TED WAS COMING OVER. The flat looked a mess.

I threw myself into a tidying and cleaning routine with terrifying and reckless speed, running around with furniture polish and a cloth and dragging the vacuum cleaner across the carpets and the wooden floors.

Next it was time for me to sort myself out. I washed quickly, shaving every part of my body that he was likely to come into contact with, and covering myself in the body lotion that I knew he loved the smell of. Then I dressed in casual clothes so it didn't look as if I'd just charged around and prepared myself for him. I wanted to look casual but beautiful...natural and glamorous all at the same time. I put on lipstick (because I didn't want to look THAT natural) and brushed my hair. The doorbell went and I looked in the mirror. Not too bad, actually, even if I said so myself.

Ted certainly seemed to think I looked OK. He charged in and grabbed me, sweeping me up into his arms; hugging and kissing me and I burst into tears. It felt like the most wonderful thing ever to happen, better, even, than when we first got together.

"Liz explained to me how bad you were feeling, and that you were confused and guilty. I understand," he said.

"But what about that text I sent?"

"I didn't get a text," he replied.

"Oh, perhaps I didn't actually send it," I said. "Phew – it didn't make any sense anyway so that's OK."

Ted was looking right into my eyes. "I was going to write 'I love you' in rose petals on the ground outside your door," he said. "I was trying to think of the most romantic thing to do. I didn't know what to do... I'm not very good at this stuff."

"You're amazing at this stuff," I said, kissing his neck.

"Bed," he replied, practically dragging me through to the bedroom and tearing at my clothes. I could feel his hands shaking as he pulled my bra straps down and cupped my breasts tenderly. He was just about to pull my trousers down and begin doing what a man and a woman do when they're on their own and feeling randy, when he stopped suddenly.

"I love you," he said. "I really love you."

"I love you too," I replied.

And after that we fell into a deep silence, punctuated only by gentle moans from me and occasional growls from him. It was all marvellous, dear reader, bloody marvellous.

8. MEETING THE FAMILY

*A*fter our initial bed-centred reunion, I explained everything to Ted, and – to his credit – he didn't judge or criticise or complain, he listened to what I had to say, nodded and told me he loved me and not to worry.

I explained all about what happened when Liz came round and he said he was proud of me for reaching out for help, but he really wished it had been him that I'd turned to. That was a good point... I didn't know why I hadn't. Perhaps Ted meant too much to me for me to make myself vulnerable and confess my emotions to him, or perhaps it was just that Liz had always told us to call her if we were in distress, so that was the call I made. Either way, Ted and I reached a really happy place. Everyone at Fat Club was delighted last week when I said that the two of us were completely back together and happier than ever. In fact, things were so great that Ted was taking me to visit his mum and dad. It felt like a huge move.

Oh, and – by the way – I went to see my GP and she was brilliant. She was going to try and get me an urgent appointment with a therapist who'd be able to help me deal with all my issues. I was feeling better and more confident than ever. Except for today. I wasn't feeling wildly confident today because of the whole 'meet the parents' thing... What if they really hated me? They might think I wasn't good enough for their precious son and the truth was – they'd probably be right.

Ted knocked on the door of their lovely semi-detached in Esher. It was a nice-looking house on a tree-lined street...very suburban, but very neat and tidy.

Ted let himself in through the front door and we wandered into the sitting room, where Ted's mum and sister were sitting. They jumped up when we walked in and rushed over to embrace Ted and shake my hand. They were both unnervingly slender and well-dressed. His mum had a real warmth about her. His sister – not so much – she was a little sour, and gave me the feeling, as she slowly looked me up and down, that she didn't like me at all.

"This is Mary," said Ted, and his mum grabbed me in a tight embrace. I was (not for the first time) embarrassed to be so large. The woman could barely get her arms around me. She felt so little and delicate. I experienced a longing to be the same way.

His sister smiled a half-smile. "Really nice to meet you," she said. "Ted has told us ALL about you, ALL the time. He never stops talking about you, to be honest. It's quite nauseating."

"Oy!" said Ted, smacking his sister.

"You're both so tiny," I said. "I'm very envious of how you keep so thin."

"You need to eat less," said his sister, bluntly. "Like Ted – he needs to eat a lot less too."

There was a horrible silence between us that no one really knew how to fill.

I felt the need to keep things light. "Well, we certainly know who eats all the pies in this house, don't we?" I said.

I didn't think the comment per se was particularly offensive...it was designed to lift the mood and add some joviality, but what made the comment offensive, and wholly inappropriate is that – exactly as I said it – Ted's dad walked into the room. I say walked, what I mean was waddled. Ted's dad was huge... I mean massive. He was probably the same size as Ted and I together.

"Someone talking about me?" asked his dad. "Someone saying that I eat all the pies?"

Shit. "No," I said. "Of course not. Definitely not. God, I'm sorry – I was talking about Ted."

"Thanks a lot," said Ted.

"No, I mean – you're a lot bigger than your mum and sister. I was only trying to be nice to your mum and sister. I'm sorry."

Ted's dad shoehorned himself into a large armchair which suddenly looked tiny beneath his massive girth.

His mum went over and removed his shoes, then pulled out the bottom part of the chair which formed a foot-rest. She lifted his legs and put them onto it. Ted's dad stared into space. I decided I didn't like him very much. Not just because I'd inadvertently insulted him, but because he seemed so different from Ted's mum. He seemed distracted and uncommunicative. Very different from my smiley, happy, chatty Ted.

"I'm sorry if that seemed offensive," I said. "I didn't see you coming, I was talking about..."

"Didn't see him coming," said Sian, Ted's sister. "How could you not see him coming? Look at the size of him."

"Oh God – they all hate me. They all hate me so much," I said to Ted, later that night when we were curled up in my bed, recalling the day with wine and slices of melon.

"No, they don't – that's just the way they are. Mum thought you were wonderful and she's the only one who counts. Dad is just miserable, and my sister is madly jealous of any woman who comes anywhere near me so you're never going to have a chance with her, but Mum – Mum is special, she's lovely, kind and wonderful and really looks after the family. She's the only one who matters, and she thinks you're great."

"Thank you," I said, and felt much better about everything.

9. SEAT BELT TRAUMAS

"Cheer up, sunshine, it might never happen."

Dave was standing in his garden looking dishevelled and filthy and absolutely bloody gorgeous. How is it that some men look better the less care they take of themselves? If Dave lived in a bin for a week he'd look like a bloody film star. He'd just get more manly and more desirable as he got stubblier and dirtier. The man reeked of masculinity. It was very distracting.

"It has already happened," I said. "I've booked my first ever driving lesson for this morning and I'm dreading it."

"Why?" asked Dave.

"Because I need to learn to drive."

"No, not – why have you booked a lesson. I meant – why are you dreading it? Learning to drive is a great thing to do."

"Because I'll be rubbish and probably crash the car and kill us all."

"No you won't – driving's easy," said Dave. "Just look around at all the idiots who can drive. If they can do it, so can you. I can even drive drunk, so it can't be that difficult."

"Ha ha," I replied.

"No, I really can," said Dave. "I did last night. Well, I say I did – I don't remember doing it, but I must have because the car is here."

"Really? You really drove home completely drunk?"

"Yep." There was a strange pride in his voice.

"You could have killed yourself." I was eager not to encourage or celebrate his reckless behaviour.

"But I didn't," he said proudly. "There's not a scratch on me."

"You could have hurt someone."

"But I didn't. I don't think so anyway. Hard to know for sure, but I don't think so or the police would have been round."

"It's not funny," I said. "Lots of people are killed by drink drivers. It's not a laughing matter at all."

"OK, killjoy, calm down. How am I supposed to get home after a few pints if I don't drive?"

"Er – walk? Get a cab? Get a train? Get a bus? Lots of options."

"I was too drunk to walk," said Dave. "Too drunk for all of those things. That's why I drove. Anyway, I'm going to bed. Good luck in your lesson. And remember – if I can do it drunk, it can't be that hard."

"No, indeed," I responded, and Dave went staggering back into his house, weaving across his small patio and stumbling through his front door.

A couple of minutes after Dave's manly frame had disappeared from view, a small yellow car appeared on the horizon, with 'Sunnyside Driving' plastered across the sides and with ridiculous primroses on the bonnet and eyelashes on the front lights. No one would be able to miss me in this thing...assuming I could get into it: my arse was bigger than the boot.

"Is it Mary?" asked the driving instructor, waving to me through the open window. He looked like he was going for his first day as a clerk at a suburban branch of Barclays. He was wearing a yellow tie to match the car and a V-neck jumper with a jacket over the top. He stepped out of the car looking slightly nervous. I noticed that his trousers were a fraction too tight...like school trousers he'd grown out of but his mum hadn't replaced.

"Yes, I'm Mary." I lifted myself off the small wall.

Standing up and sitting down are two of the things I find hardest to do as a fatty. I had to use my hands to lever myself off the wall, and as I leaned forward, my protruding stomach got in the way. The other thing I hate is doing my shoelaces. The agony of leaning over to do anything, anything at all, when you're heavy cannot be overstated. I feel a wave of nausea and sickness wash through me whenever I bend over, as if my stomach is pushing up against all my internal organs and stopping them from working properly.

I waddled towards the car and the driving instructor shook my hand and told me to get into the passenger seat.

"We'll head out to a disused shopping centre car park and have a chat and get started," he said. "That way there'll be no pressure and no one to see you. OK?"

"OK," I said and felt massively relieved. The guy seemed calm and in control, and I liked the idea of going to learn in an old disused car park rather than on the road. Nothing could go wrong if I was miles from other people and cars. Could it?

I sat down heavily in the seat and the whole car felt like it had dropped beneath me – like a fat kid sitting on the see-saw.

"Seat belt on then," he said.

Ah.

I pulled the seat belt as slowly as I could, hoping that it was long enough to go round me, but it jolted to a stop a considerable way short. Damn. I pulled again, ever so slowly in case the reason it had stopped was because it had got caught up or triggered the stop mechanism, but – no – it had stopped because that was the end of it. The seat belt didn't get any longer. I was too fat for the seat belt. It was mortifying.

"All done up?" asked the driving instructor, unaware of the crushing few seconds I'd just endured.

"Yes," I replied, tucking the seat belt down beside my thigh, and pretending it was done up.

"OK, I want you to watch me as I drive, then we'll be talking about it when we get to the car park. See how the first thing I do is to put the key into the ignition and turn it." He did this and the car immediately started beeping like we were out of petrol or something.

"Ah, that beeping is to say that the seat belts aren't done up. Can you check yours is properly clicked in," he said.

Oh hell. This is horrible.

"Yep, all clicked in," I replied. But I could see that this strategy wasn't going to get me very far. He was going to start investigating.

"Are you sure?" he asked.

"Yes, all fine. Just drive."

"I can't drive while the emergency warning light's on. It means one of the seat belts isn't done up properly and that could be extremely dangerous."

Oh for God's sake, man.

"We're not travelling far though, are we? Let's just go," I said.

But Mr Health & Safety was out of the car and over to my side of the car to examine the seat belt situation.

"Oh it's not done up at all!" he said. "Look, can you see? It's not plugged in, that's what the problem is."

Silly me.

Then he started pulling it and fiddling with the seat belt container, trying to work out why the seat belt wouldn't go in and end the interminable bleeping that was still belting away inside the little car.

"It seems shorter this side than the other, I can't get enough of it to come out," he said, baffled. Bless him. Could he not see that I was fucking huge and that it simply wasn't big enough to go round me? We could blame the seat belt all we wanted, but the truth was that I was so large that a conventional seat belt wouldn't go round me. It wasn't the first time this had happened, and I was sure it wouldn't be the last, but it was still mortifying.

I could see my poor, dear driving instructor suddenly working out what had happened. I could see it in his body language as he pulled himself up short, and stood with his hands on his hips, looking down. I also sensed that this was probably the worst thing that had ever happened to him. It was like he felt personally responsible for the fact that the seat belt didn't work, even though it was entirely my fault.

He had no idea what to do. On one hand there was his absolute horror of having to tell me that I was too fat for his seat belt; on the other hand, there was his absolute horror of breaking any of the rules of the road – so he didn't want to drive off with me unable to wear a seat belt. If he'd had any more hands, I imagined that on the third one there would be the issue of him not wanting to lose my business. The invisible third hand won, he got back into his side of the car and off we went, in search of an empty car park so that the fat girl could drive around without killing anyone.

When we reached the car park there were children playing football at the far side of it.

"Be careful," the instructor screamed out of the window. "Learner driver here…"

"I'll be fine," I told him, but the instructor didn't look as if he thought it was going to be at all fine. He was gripping onto the sides of the door as he encouraged me to look in my mirror before moving off, then he told me to keep looking in the mirror. "It's the most important thing," he said, though I didn't think that looking behind me could be that important, could it? I felt I was using the mirror so much that I was looking backwards more than I was looking forwards. And all the while, the beeping noise was going on, driving me nuts as I tried to concentrate on driving in a straight line while looking in the mirror. It seemed unlikely I was going to be a natural at driving.

10. DODGY DRIVING AND AN ANGRY POLICEMAN

"I could easily teach you to drive," said Dave. "Easily."

I was sitting on the top step with my head in my hands, shaking my head forlornly.

"Don't worry about the driving instructor," he added. "Really, it's easy."

"But everything went wrong, Dave. I mean EVERYTHING. I couldn't get the fucking seat belt on, then my feet wouldn't touch the pedals unless I had the seat all the way forward and then it was so far forward that my stomach was in the way when I tried to reach down to put the key in the ignition. It was all an embarrassing disaster. Honestly, Dave, the biggest disaster you can imagine. I'm not cut out for driving. I don't know what I am cut out for, all I know is that it's not driving."

"Yes you are, everyone can drive. You can drive, I can teach you to drive – driving is easy. You know what, mate, I'm not great at much: I can get girls to drop their knickers at my door and I can drive. There's no question that I can teach you to drive, so get in the seat and let's get going."

Dave insisted that I needed to be in the driving seat, and that we weren't going to a deserted car park. "We'll just get going, everything will be fine," he insisted. He was an absolute darling to make the effort to teach me, but to be honest, I didn't hold out great deal of hope. In fact, ignore that, I didn't hold out any hope at all.

The good news was, Dave had no complicated beeping situation going on and no lights that flash when I failed to connect the seat belt.

"OK, what do I do first?" I asked.

"We need to get going, sweetheart," he said. "Put the key in ignition and let's get this baby moving."

His was an altogether less sophisticated an approach to the one I'd endured with the driving instructor.

"Turn the key then." I did as I was told and edged the car forward on Dave's command, juddering and faltering as it hopped along like a bunny rabbit.

"OK," said Dave. "So we're moving, but now can we drive it so it's like a car and not like a fucking woodland creature."

"OK, how do I do that?"

"Didn't the driving instructor tell you?"

"No, we didn't get that far."

"How far did you get then?" he asked. "I mean – if driving for a bit in a straight line wasn't touched upon, what exactly were you doing?"

"We were doing things like mirror, signal, manoeuvre," I said.

"Oh yes, yes, yes you need to do that. I forgot about all that stuff. Yes, do that as well…before you start driving around."

"OK." I was really starting to wonder now whether Dave was absolutely the right person to be teaching me to drive.

Still, we set off, with me trying to remember everything the driving instructor said about mirror, signal, manoeuvre, and how to proceed cautiously and keep looking in the mirror to make sure cyclists aren't passing and to make sure you know what cars are behind you. Dave seemed strangely unaware of these simple rules of the road.

One thing I was really struggling with was driving a different car to the one the previous day. I didn't know how you were supposed to remember how much force to use in different cars. The driving instructor's car was completely different from Dave's car – it was somehow slower, everything took a little longer. It meant that when I turned the wheel in Dave's car with the sort of force I used in the instructor's, the car went up and onto the pavement until I brought it to a juddering halt within inches of a lamppost.

"Well." Dave grabbed the steering wheel and redirected it back onto the road. "That wasn't great. And just as I was starting to think you were getting the hang of it. And slow down, for goodness' sake, why are you going so fast? It's like being in a car with Lewis Hamilton."

"OK, I'll try," I said, once firmly back on solid ground and driving at a sensible speed.

"You're still going too fast; you have to slow down," said Dave. "Slow right down... You need to slow down, Mary."

"I am going slowly."

"No, you're not," said Dave. We approached a zebra crossing as someone walked out, so I slammed on the brakes, sending both of us flying forward so we had to put our hands out to stop ourselves careering through the windscreen. I had no seat belt on because I was terrifyingly fat, and Dave had no seat belt on out of some inexplicable sympathy with me (he'd said, "I won't wear one either then." A decision he was coming to bitterly regret).

"What was that for?" said Dave with considerable aggression. "I told you to slow down earlier. You can't just drive full pelt and put your brakes on at the last minute, it's not fair on the drivers behind you and it's not fair to those walking across the zebra crossing. Also, it's not fair to me. I'm a bloody nervous wreck here, doll face. Now slow down."

"OK, OK."

"Go on then, the traffic is waiting behind."

I wasn't very good at starting yet, so I put my foot flat down on the pedal and the car leaped forward.

"Bring the car to the side of the road," Dave said, in measured tones. He sounded quite scared now.

"Sorry?"

"I want you to park the car at the side of the road."

Parking was something we hadn't done yet, so I brought the car to an emergency stop.

"Not in the middle of the road," said Dave, pointing towards the curb while holding his head in the other hand.

"I don't really know about bringing the car into the curb," I replied. "If you remember, you're supposed to be teaching me how to do all this stuff."

"OK, turn the steering wheel towards the curb, put your foot down on the accelerator gently and it will go towards the curb... It's not that hard."

"OK, I'll give it a go."

Anyway, that was how we ended up with the car half on the pavement and half on the road, and Dave instructing me to reverse off the pavement back into the road.

"I've never done reversing before," I said. "Where is the reverse button?"

"Oh God," he said, as he began to talk me through the process of reversing, telling me to put my foot down on the clutch as he moved the gear stick to reverse. I then put my foot down on the accelerator in a manner that I believed to be gentle, but was clearly more aggressive than it should have been. The car flew back. I braked suddenly and Dave and I went shooting forward. I bashed my head on the steering wheel which emitted a loud beep.

"Don't beep the horn," he said. "You're bringing enough attention to us as it is."

"I didn't beep the horn," I said. "My head hit the horn when I went flying in my seat."

"OK then, well you better move us forward a bit, you're sticking out into the road and the cars can't get past."

I suppose it was inevitable, really, but the next car to come along was a police car. "For the love of Christ," said Dave, as the panda car pulled alongside me and the officer wound down his window. "Everything OK?" The police officer gave a dramatic raise of his eyebrows as he spoke, indicating that, to his mind at least, things were far from OK.

"I'm sorry, officer, I'm learning to drive," I said. "It's harder than it looks, isn't it?"

"Indeed it is," said the officer. "For starters you should have L-plates on the car."

"I forgot to put them on," said Dave. "I will put them on next time we come out."

The officer didn't look convinced, but he could see we were in a perilous situation, and he needed to leave us so I could remove the car from its position, sitting diagonally across the road. So he just nodded and said, "Make sure you do."

And at this stage – I promise you – everything was OK. All we had to do was get out of the ridiculous position I'd got us into, and continue on our journey. But Dave, being Dave, couldn't let it lie like that...

"Dickhead," he said, thinking the policeman was out of earshot. But the policeman wasn't out of earshot. He reversed the car back alongside my car and looked over at Dave. "Sorry, did you say something?" he asked.

And this was when I made the biggest cock-up ever. I figured it would be good to diffuse the situation with a light-hearted joke. Big mistake.

"Honestly, officer, he had three pints at lunchtime – you can't talk to him when he's like this." I looked over at Dave and nudged him playfully.

"She's joking," he said plaintively.

"Of course I'm joking." I looked back at the policeman who was getting out of his car and coming round to open the door.

"Get out," he instructed, all of the gentleness having gone from his voice.

"OK, officer." I stepped out of the car.

"Why aren't you wearing your seat belt?"

"I was," I lied. "I took it off when you came up alongside us."

"OK, you get out of the car too," he said to Dave. "And blow into this..."

The police officer handed Dave a breathalyser.

"I'm not blowing into that," said Dave. "Not without my lawyer present."

"Dave, just blow into it," I said. Then I turned to the officer: "Really, I was just joking, this is getting way out of hand... It was a little joke."

"It wasn't funny. Drink-driving is serious."

"You'll have to take me to the station, I'm not blowing into that bag," said Dave. Honestly, this was getting way out of line. It really was just a little silly joke and now Dave was refusing to blow into the tester thing, the policeman was getting very agitated, and everyone was getting angry and cross with one another.

"Mary, can you call my lawyer on this number..."

He handed me a piece of paper with 'I can't blow into that thing, I've been drinking all morning,' written on it. What the hell were we supposed to do now?

"I was joking," I said to the officer. "This is going to look ridiculous when it all goes to court and I say I was making a little joke and you took it way too seriously. The police have a bad enough reputation for being hard-headed at the best of times. I'm really sorry I made a joke...it was in poor taste. I promise I'll never make a joke like that again."

"OK, OK," said the police officer. He turned to Dave: "Make sure you get those L-plates."

"I will," said Dave, and the officer drove off.

"Bloody hell!" I walked towards Dave. "You were drinking this morning?"

"Yes." He wrapped his arms around me as we clung to one another in relief.

"But you can't drink drive."

"I didn't drink drive. You were driving."

"Oh, bloody hell," I said. "You're such an idiot."

Behind us there was traffic chaos. Cars were beeping and drivers had got out and were standing on the road shouting at us to "move the f**king car."

"I better move it." I extracted myself from Dave's arms...he'd been holding on to me way longer than I'd expected him to.

We got into the car. I reversed out and nearly hit three people, Dave held his head in his hands and people all around us shouted angrily.

LATER THAT NIGHT, TED PHONED. HE'D BEEN DUE TO COME ROUND FOR the evening, but said he wasn't feeling well.

"Oh no, sorry about that," I said.

"What did you do today?" he asked.

"Nothing much." I couldn't possibly tell him about the driving lesson. He'd have a fit if he thought I'd done a driving lesson with a drunk bloke.

"See anyone?" he asked.

I decided not to mention Downstairs Dave.

"No," I said. "I just hung around at home and did some chores. How about you?"

"I have to go," he said, and he disappeared from the line.

Poor thing, he sounded really unwell.

11. HUGGING DAVE

I woke in the morning to a text from Ted.

"Are you awake?" it said.

"Yes," I replied.

A minute later my phone rang.

"This is awkward," he said. "It's awkward and it's fucking awful."

"What's happened?"

"I know that you and Dave are having an affair," he said. "Don't deny it because I know for sure."

I sat up in bed. "What the hell are you talking about? Of course I'm not having an affair with him or anyone else – I'm in love with you."

"My sister saw you," he said.

"She didn't."

"She did."

"No, she didn't, because I'm not having an affair with him. It must have been someone else. To be honest, Ted, I've seen a lot of women go in and out of his flat – it could be any one of them."

"Don't lie, Mary," he said, and I could hear how deadly serious he was.

"Ted, I promise you, I'm not having an affair with Dave. I don't know how to make it any clearer."

"Then explain this," he said, and my phone bleeped to tell me there was a text. I went into my texts and retrieve one from Ted. It consisted of a picture…of Dave and me with our arms wrapped round each other, caught up in a huge hug. Oh God. It looked really dodgy.

"Have you got it?" asked Ted.

"Yes."

"You told me you'd spent all your time in the house doing chores, so you're lying to me. I can only assume you lied because you're seeing Dave. Thanks very much."

"No, no, it's not like that," I tried.

"So, you didn't lie to me?"

"Well, yes I did, but not because I'm having an affair. I lied because Dave gave me a driving lesson and I discovered afterwards – after the police stopped us, but that's another story – I discovered afterwards that he'd been drinking all morning. Look, Dave's an idiot and I shouldn't have got him to teach me to drive, but he offered and I really want to learn."

"Why didn't you ask me?" said Ted. "Why do you always turn to other people for help?"

"Because I don't want to look an idiot in front of you."

"And it doesn't look like much driving's going on in the picture… you've obviously been kissing him."

"No. I hugged him in relief because the police didn't arrest him."

"This is all ridiculous," said Ted. "I'm going now."

"No, don't go," I said. "Ted, I love you. This is all a silly mix-up."

But it was too late. Ted had gone and I was left holding my phone on which there was a picture of Dave and me in an embrace. Oh God. There was only one woman to call at a time like this.

I dialled Charlie's number. Luckily, she was in and answered straight away.

"Send me the picture," she told me, when I'd explained my predicament.

"Mmmm…that's not great," she said. "What are you going to do?"

"I've no idea," I said. "That's why I'm calling you."

"Probably time for an old-fashioned committee meeting, don't you think?"

"Blimey, we haven't done one of those for ages."

We always used to call a committee meeting if one of us was struggling with something (usually involving a man). All the girls would descend on the stricken woman's house and they would jointly work out what was the best course of action.

"Your place, tonight at 6pm, I'll let the girls know. See you later."

See – I told you Charlie would be the right person to talk to.

THERE WAS WINE, THERE WERE LOW-CALORIE, FAT-FREE NIBBLES, AND fresh flowers filled the room with a soft, rose scent. I was all prepared, but feeling dreadful. I really didn't want to lose Ted. Charlie nodded her approval as she surveyed the scene and helped herself to a cheese puff.

"Don't worry, angel, we'll sort this out," she said.

"I hope so. I'm such an idiot."

I put some music on and read through the agenda I prepared in advance of this key tactical and strategic meeting.

It was headed 'operation MATT' (Mary and Ted together), followed by the list of people who'd be there later: me, Charlie, Janice and Veronica from Fat Club, and Sandra the beautician whose arms I cried in when I bumped into her on the High Street that afternoon. To be honest, I think she was just relieved that she hadn't received a legal letter after she'd turned my skin the colour of boiled beetroot. Anything else was a bonus.

1. Convince Ted that Mary still likes him
2. Convince Ted that Mary is trustworthy, and that nothing happened with Downstairs Dave
3. Approach Ted's sister?
4. Infiltrate Ted's friend group to convince them that Ted and Mary should be together

5. Get Ted and Mary together whenever possible
6. Drop lots of hints to Ted about how great the two of them are together

OBVIOUSLY AT THE END THERE WOULD BE TIME FOR ANY OTHER Business, and there would be someone taking notes and making sure that all the things talked about got implemented by the people in the group. There would be follow-up meetings, more strategising, and regular catch-ups to make sure that everything discussed at the meeting was properly and effectively implemented. It wasn't exactly the United Nations, but it wasn't far off.

The girls began to arrive, streaming into my house, taking a glass of wine and chatting amiably while we all collected in the front room. Madonna sang out from the stereo as hands disappeared into bowls of low-fat crisps, and glasses were replenished.

"Right, if everyone could take a seat, we can begin," said Charlie, taking the lead and addressing the assembled guests. "We have a terrible situation on our hands. Our lovely Mary has managed to behave like a giant buffoon, and spent time in the company of dodgy Downstairs Dave, henceforth to be referred to as Double D. Their liaison has come to Ted's knowledge, and he has told Mary that he is unhappy, a small argument ensued and now Mary and Ted have split up. The purpose of today's meeting is to work out how to get them back together again."

"What have you done so far?" asked Sandra, as she finished her wine and laid her glass on the table.

I reached out to refill her glass. "I haven't really done anything," I confessed. "I don't really know what to do."

"Tell us what happened," she said.

"Well, Dave offered to teach me to drive, I thought it would be a really good idea, because the day before I'd had a terrible driving lesson. Dave said he was a good teacher. Turns out he is a really crap teacher and a really crap driver, the whole thing was a disaster. He nearly went into shock when I mounted the curb, and he was rude to a police officer, then I told the police officer that he was drunk, then he refused to blow into the breathalyser because it turns out he *was* drunk, then we were so relieved when the policeman went away that we hugged. I didn't realise that Ted sister had seen me and taken a picture which she showed to Ted."

"Oh," said Sandra. "What a pickle."

"You mean what a bitch," said Veronica. "I mean – really? That's such a tosser-ish thing to do."

"It is," said Charlie. "His sister knows nothing about what's going on and decides to intervene. She just doesn't like Mary."

"But I can't slag off the sister to Ted, the two of them are very close, and he is sure that his sister was simply acting in his best interests," I explained.

"OK," said Janice. "The first question, then, what did you say to Ted?"

"I told him the truth," I replied, smiling inwardly with pride. I'm the sort of person who always manages to make a mountain out of a molehill...the sort of person who opens her mouth and makes everything 50 times worse. But, on this occasion, I didn't seem to have done that. I'd just told the truth.

"And what did Ted say?"

"He was sceptical. He didn't understand why I'd lied originally about it...which I hadn't...I just didn't tell him the whole truth which, as everyone knows, is different from lying."

"OK, OK," said Charlie. "Enough of what has happened. What are we going to do to put it all right again? Has everyone got an agenda? Let's bring this meeting to order."

There was a shuffling sound as everyone picked up their papers.

"OK, first item on the agenda – convince Ted that Mary still likes him. How are we going to do that?"

"I'm friends with him on Facebook," said Janice. "I could send him a note on there. I could just say that I'm checking he's OK, and that I'm sorry that he and Mary have split up, because I know how much she loves him."

"Good. Excellent. Anyone else?"

"I'll talk to him at Fat Club," said Veronica. "I'll pull him aside and make sure he knows how much she likes him."

"Good." Charlie struck off item one on her agenda. "Now, what's next?"

"Convince Ted that nothing happened with Downstairs Dave," said Janice. "Well, I can do that when I chat to him on Facebook. We don't want too many people approaching him, he might suspect that it's all planned."

"He'll never suspect that we have a bloody working party set up though, will he. Men would never think of doing something like this," said Sandra with a snort. Oh God, she was very drunk. "You know what we should do – get Downstairs Dave to join us. Maybe he'll be able to give us a man's perspective on the whole thing? Or perhaps he'll offer to talk to Ted."

"No, I don't want him talking to Ted," I said.

"Might not be a bad idea to have a male point of view, though," offered Charlie. "I mean – if we just invite him up for a glass of wine and pick his brains for 15 minutes, that would be OK, wouldn't it?"

"I guess so." I wasn't wholly convinced that we needed a male point of view, and I didn't feel great about DD – the cause of all the anguish – being in my flat, but it was decided that he really should contribute to the meeting, so Charlie rushed off to find him and I pondered the situation.

"What if Ted finds that he was here?" I said. "I mean – this could make everything worse."

"If he finds out that DD is here, just tell him that you invited him so you could get a male point of view at the planning evening."

"Yes, but then I'll have to tell him about the planning evening. He'll think I've lost my mind if he knows about what's happening tonight."

"Good point," Janice conceded. "He can't know about any of this or he'll have you carted off to a mental home."

On that note, Downstairs Dave walked into the room and there was an audible sigh as all the women swooned in his wake. He did look lovely...really sexy and dishevelled as always. I finished my glass of wine and steadied myself by gripping hold of the mantelpiece as he leaned over and planted a kiss on my cheek. Well, I say 'cheek', but I turned round suddenly and he caught me on the lips by mistake (yes – mistake!), and there was another audible sigh from the girls in the room as they all contemplated the idea of being kissed by Dave…he really was a spectacularly good-looking man.

"You need to help us," said Charlie, as Dave took handfuls of peanuts and rocketed them into his mouth by slapping his hand up against his lips. "We need to get Mary and Ted back together."

"The fat guy?" said Dave, looking at me.

"Yes."

"Cool. He seems nice. Why don't you tell him you want to go out with him?"

"Well, we were going out together, then he saw me with you, when you were giving me a driving lesson, and he thought something was going on with us, so the relationship ended."

"He thought something was going on with us? With you and me? Really?"

"Yes, his sister saw us. Do you remember when the policeman left and we had a hug? She got the wrong idea, told him and he thinks we're having an affair."

"Just tell him we're not," he said. "Just keep saying it…every time you see him. Don't play silly games and get your friends to drop hints – just tell him the truth. Be honest and straightforward. You haven't done anything wrong."

We all looked shell-shocked. Dave leaned over and picked up my phone, playing with it as he talked.

"But we've got a complicated plan."

"You don't need a complicated plan – just tell him the truth."

Just tell him? Really? It couldn't be that simple.

12. ROSE PETALS ON THE BREEZE

So...once again I was sitting at home wondering how to apologise to Ted. It was becoming quite a regular thing in my life. This time I felt like I had to phone him, rather than text. It would be wrong to text, so I picked up my mobile. I'd been thinking about this all night...since the meeting when Dave was so adamant that I should talk and not play games.

"Hello," he said, all jolly. "Cheered up now?"

"No," I said, miserably. "Why would I have cheered up?"

"Have you been outside today?" he asked.

"No, I haven't. Look, Ted. I really love you. I don't want us to split up."

"Where are you?" he asked. "I mean – have you left the house yet?"

"No," I replied. "I'm still in my pyjamas... I can't face work."

"Open the front door."

"Why?"

"Just do it," he said.

"OK."

I walked up to the door and swung it open, and there, in front of my house was 'I love you' written out in rose petals.

"Oh God," I said. "That's so lovely. Oh Ted, that's lovely. Why did you do that? I thought you hated me. You thought I was having an affair with Dave."

"I don't hate you. Dave called me yesterday night," explained Ted. "He told me he'd taken my number out of your phone and wanted to talk to me to tell me what happened. Turns out he's a pretty decent guy. I'm sorry I didn't believe you. It's just – you know – I was hurt and scared. I don't want to lose you."

"I don't want to lose you." I bent down to gather up some of the rose petals.

"I love you," he said. "I'll always love you."

And every care in the world drifted away on the breeze, followed by dozens of pale pink rose petals.

"Come round," I said.

"I'm on my way," he replied.

ENDS

I REALLY HOPE YOU HAVE ENJOYED READING ABOUT MARY BROWN. IF you have, there are loads more Adorable Fat Girl books for you to try, as she goes off on holiday, receives a mysterious invitation and tries online dating.

There's also a romance series and a 'Wags' series.

You can find out more about all the books here:

https://bernicebloom.com/

Or just click on the links below

THANK YOU SO MUCH FOR BUYING THE BOOK.

BB xxx

. . .

BOOK ONE: Diary of an Adorable Fat Girl

Mary Brown is funny, gorgeous and bonkers. She's also about six stone overweight. When she realises she can't cross her legs, has trouble bending over to tie her shoelaces without wheezing like an elderly chain-smoker, and discovers that even her hands and feet look fat, it's time to take action. But what action? She's tried every diet under the sun.

This is the story of what happens when Mary joins 'Fat Club' where she meets a cast of funny characters and one particular man who catches her eye.

CLICK HERE:

My Book

BOOK TWO: Adventures of an Adorable Fat Girl

Mary can't get into any of the dresses in Zara (she tries and fails. It's messy!). Still, what does she care? She's got a lovely new boyfriend whose thighs are bigger than her's (yes!!!) and all is looking well...except when she accidentally gets herself into several thousand pounds worth of trouble at the silent auction, has to eat her lunch under the table in the pub because Ted's workmates have spotted them, and suffers the indignity of having a young man's testicles dangled into her face on a party boat to Amsterdam. Oh, and then there are all the issues with the hash-cakes and the sex museum. Besides all those things - everything's fine...just fine!

CLICK HERE:

My Book

BOOK THREE: Crazy Life of an Adorable Fat Girl

The second course of 'Fat Club' starts and Mary reunites with the cast of funny characters who graced book one. But this time there's a new Fat Club member...a glamorous blonde who Mary takes against.

We also see Mary facing troubles in her relationship with the wonderful Ted, and we discover why she has been suffering from an eating disorder for most of her life. What traumatic incident in Mary's past has caused her all these problems?

The story is tender and warm, but also laugh-out-loud funny. It will resonate with anyone who has dieted, tried to keep up with any sort of exercise programme or spent 10 minutes in a changing room trying to extricate herself from a way too-small garment that she ambitiously tried on and is now completely stuck in.

CLICK HERE:

My Book

BOOK FOUR: FIRST THREE BOOKS COMBINED

This is the first three Fat Girl books altogether in one fantastic, funny package

CLICK HERE:

My Book

BOOK FIVE: Christmas with Adorable Fat Girl

It's the Adorable Fat Girl's favourite time of year and she embraces it with the sort of thrill and excitement normally reserved for toddlers seeing jelly tots. Our funny, gorgeous and bonkers heroine finds herself dancing from party to party, covered in tinsel, decorating the Beckhams' Christmas tree, dressing up as Father Christmas, declaring live on This Morning that she's a drug addict and enjoying two Christmas lunches in quick succession. She's the party queen as she stumbles wildly from disaster to disaster. A funny little treasure to see you smiling through the festive period.

CLICK HERE:

My Book

BOOK SIX: Adorable Fat Girl shares her Weight Loss Tips

As well as having a crazy amount of fun at Fat Club, Mary also loses weight...a massive 40lbs!! How does she do it? Here in this mini book - for the first time - she describes the rules that helped her. Also included are the stories of readers who have written in to share their weight loss stories. This is a kind approach to weight loss. It's about learning to love yourself as you shift the pounds. It worked for Mary

Brown and everyone at Fat Club (even Ted who can't go a day without a bag of chips and thinks a pint isn't a pint without a bag of pork scratchings). I hope it works for you, and I hope you enjoy it.

CLICK HERE My Book

BOOK SEVEN: Adorable Fat Girl on Safari

Mary Brown, our fabulous, full-figured heroine, is off on safari with an old school friend. What could possibly go wrong? Lots of things, it turns out. Mary starts off on the wrong foot by turning up dressed in a ribbon bedecked bonnet, having channeled Meryl Streep from Out of Africa. She falls in lust with a khaki-clad ranger half her age and ends up stuck in a tree wearing nothing but her knickers, while sandwiched between two inquisitive baboons. It's never dull...

CLICK HERE:

My Book

BOOK EIGHT: Cruise with an Adorable Fat Girl

Mary is off on a cruise. It's the trip of a lifetime...featuring eat-all-you-can

buffets and a trek through Europe with a 96-year-old widower called Frank and a

flamboyant Spanish dancer called Juan Pedro. Then there's the desperately

handsome captain, the appearance of an ex-boyfriend on the ship, the time she's

mistaken for a Hollywood film star in Lisbon and tonnes of clothes shopping all

over Europe.

CLICK HERE:

My Book

BOOK NINE: Adorable Fat Girl Takes up Yoga

The Adorable Fat Girl needs to do something to get fit. What about yoga? I mean - really - how hard can that be? A bit of chanting, some toe touching and a new leotard. Easy! She signs up for a weekend retreat, packs up assorted snacks and heads for the country-side to get in touch with her chi and her third eye. And that's when it all goes wrong. Featuring frantic chickens, an unexpected mud bath, men in loose-fitting shorts and no pants, calamitous headstands, a new bizarre friendship with a yoga guru and a quick hospital trip.

CLICK HERE:

My Book

BOOK TEN: The first three holiday books combined

This is a combination book containing three of the books in my holiday series: Adorable Fat Girl on Safari, Cruise with an Adorable Fat Girl and Adorable Fat Girl takes up Yoga.

CLICK HERE:

My Book

BOOK ELEVEN: Adorable Fat Girl and the Mysterious Invitation

Mary Brown receives an invitation to a funeral. The only problem is: she has absolutely no idea who the guy who's died is. She's told that the deceased invited her on his deathbed, and he's very keen for her to attend, so she heads off to a dilapidated old farm house in a remote part of Wales. When she gets there, she discovers that only five other people have been invited to the funeral. None of them knows who he is either.

NO ONE GOING TO THIS FUNERAL HAS EVER HEARD OF THE DECEASED.

Then they are told that they have 20 hours to work out why they have been invited in order to inherit a million pounds.

Who is this guy and why are they there? And what of the ghostly goings on in the ancient old building?

CLICK HERE:

My Book

BOOK TWELVE Adorable Fat Girl goes to weight loss camp

Mary Brown heads to Portugal for a weight loss camp and discovers it's nothing like she expected. "I thought it would be Slimming World in the sunshine, but this is bloody torture," she says, after boxing, running, sand training (sand training?), more running, more star jumps and eating nothing but carrots. Mary wants to hide from the instructors and cheat the system. The trouble is, her mum is with her, and won't leave her alone for a second. Then there's the angry instructor with the deep, dark secret about why he left the army; and the mysterious woman who sneaks into their pool and does synchronised swimming every night. Who the hell is she? Why's she in their pool? And what about Yvonne - the slim, attractive lady who disappears every night after dinner. Where's she going? And what unearthly difficulties will Mary get herself into when she decides to follow her to find out...

CLICK HERE:

My Book

BOOK THIRTEEN: The first two weight loss books:

This is Weight loss tips and Weight loss camp together

CLICK HERE:

My Book

BOOK FOURTEEN: Adorable Fat Girl goes online dating

She's big, beautiful and bonkers, and now she's going online dating. Buckle up and prepare for trouble, laughter and total chaos.

Mary Brown is gorgeous, curvaceous and wants to find a boyfriend.

But where's she going to meet someone new? She doesn't want to hang around pubs all evening (actually that bit's not true), and she doesn't want to have to get out of her pyjamas unless really necessary (that bit's true).

There's only one thing for it - she will launch herself majestically onto the dating scene.

Aided and abetted by her friends, including Juan Pedro and best friend Charlie, Mary heads out on NINE DATES IN NINE DAYS.

She meets an interesting collection of men, including those she nicknames: Usain Bolt, Harry the Hoarder, and Dead Wife Darren.

Then just when she thinks things can't get any worse, Juan organises a huge, entirely inadvisable party at the end.

It's internet dating like you've never known it before...
CLICK HERE:
My Book

BOOK FIFTEEN: The Official Handbook for Adorable Fat Girls

This is the Ultimate Guide to being an Adorable Fat Girl. A reference book packed with life-changing advice, and some basic rules for coping in a thin world.

For example What is being fat?

Being fat is...

- Hearing the intake of breath when you sit down on someone's new deckchair. They smile, but their eyes are screaming 'For the love of God, don't sit on that. It's new and I love it and you're the size of a baby elephant and likely to rip it in two.'
- Enjoying the warm cry: "Lose some weight lardarse" as you walk down the street. Yes, that's right - life advice from passing van drivers. Excellent. Just what we all need, a bit of drive-by counselling. And the thing is - it works perfectly...as soon as someone shouts that out, I'm really inspired to go to step aerobics and eat nothing but air-dried vegetables and grated ice cubes for the next week. NOT.
- Dealing with chaffing. We'll deal with this more a little later, but - my God - how much does it hurt? As if someone has

ground smashed glass into your inner thighs before coating them with vinegar
- Fearing any occasion when you may be asked to wear a seatbelt, life jacket, or harness of any kind. It won't fit. Take a look at your harness and then a quick look at my arse. How in God's name are you going to get that child-sized device over this lorry-sized body. Don't make me try. Find a bigger one.

The book has a range of sections including coping with shopping, travelling, exercise, dating and the summer... There's also a section on the issue of being overweight at work,,along with the results of an EXCLUSIVE SURVEY conducted for this book. The results and stories are staggering.

Some of the sections are funny, some are serious, some are packed with advice, others are packed with sympathy. It's your indispensable guide to coping with life in a thin world.

CLICK HERE:
My Book

SUNSHINE COTTAGE BOOKS

Also read Bernice's romantic fiction in the Sunshine Cottage series about the Lopez girls, based in gorgeous Cove Bay, Carolina.
CLICK HERE:
My Book

-

THE WAGS BOOKS

Met Tracie Martin, the crazy Wag with a mission to change the world...
CLICK HERE:

Wag's Diary
My Book

Wags in LA
My Book

Wags at the World Cup
My Book